LOVE IN THE TIME OF TERROR

by Mary Faderan

ISBN:
978-0-692-083785-8

Chapter One

Dear Mom,

I'm writing you from my new pad here in London. It's got a posh address, a little on the shabby side but the area is clean - a bit up in the snob appeal. I'm sharing it with a woman who needs to use it only on some weekends. She's letting me pay it cheaply mostly because I'll be taking over the lease when she gets herself married in a month

I live in Charing Cross, the one area that's pretty famous. There's a hospital nearby, where I have my job. I like it enough. People seem nice enough, but I've not a chance to get to know any of them. There are three of us including Mr. Ham. His admin is Mrs. Bellingham – she's a mature lady. Then our secretary is Miss Orsay who is around my age, but she isn't really into chatting with newbies like me, it seems. I've got another social worker coworker, Marjorie Stitz, but she works part-time since she has a little kid and has no husband. I've got the same sort of job like when I worked at home - social worker. I don't know a lot about the area yet, but I will be making my tour of the place today.

About Cor, I've broken up with him. I know you and Daddy will be pleased about that. Cor and I weren't suited for each other. Don't worry, we never to the altar. He just got into too much trouble with his gambling, and then he found someone with money which stole him away from me. I couldn't put up with it all, so I left him two weeks ago.

I'm staying with a woman who is subletting her apartment, and I'll be taking over the lease once she and her fiancé get married.

If Daddy wants to visit here, I'd love it. I think he's so famous now any hospital will ask him to be a visiting professor or as guest speaker at some conference they always put up these days in the hospitals.

I like the idea of living in London. I never thought I'd end up here - but I don't miss Connecticut much. Although parts of Connecticut are like some of the countrysides in England, not that much because there are rolling, green, hills, meadows, and not as many big trees that bother you when you go for a drive, as far as I've seen. There are lovely cottages with thatched roofs, and then there are the lakes where they call it The Lake District, haha.

The flat has two bedrooms, with chintz curtains and an efficient kitchen. I'm sitting in it now, having some coffee. I like tea, but it will take time to get to be a tea drinker. I have to say goodbye for now. Don't be sad about the breakup. Well, I know you will think it's a good thing, but I know you'll be worried about me. Don't worry it will be ok. I'll see how life is like in London and how the work goes. I think being a social worker here will be great – lots of people here need help – lots of diversity and many who are poor and depending on government charity.

Love,

Rebecca

The writer of the email paused at her keyboard

and sipped her mug of hot coffee. It was a Saturday

morning, and her day started earlier at about 4 a.m. She

was still in her bedroom slippers although she wore her

leggings and slouchy, shaker stitch sweater. Her face

was clear of makeup, although she hardly wore any as a

rule. Her hair, slightly tousled, with honey blonde hues,

curled loosely around her shoulders. She tried to feel

upbeat, but there was a feeling of excitement and fear

remained. Rebecca, at 28 years of age, was going

through a new life after the breakup two weeks ago, of

her engagement to Ralph Corcoran. They met in

Connecticut where they both worked at Yale-New

Haven Hospital. He was a surgical resident under her

father, and she worked in the Social Work department.

Cor was British and took her hastily a couple of months

ago to marry in London.

She was now single again. Her shoulders

shivered a bit at the thought. Her face was sober as she regarded the view from the kitchen window. It was all she could do to keep her doubts at life alone at bay. She faced a decision to live in a new country, a new city. Her worries became large as she considered the loss of the solidity of Cor's presence.

The phone rang, and she picked it up. "Hello."

"It's Cor. How are you, Rebecca?"

She frowned. "Fine. What are you calling me for?"

"I wanted to hear your voice. I haven't seen you for two weeks, sweet girl. What about meeting me for a late breakfast somewhere?"

"I don't know why. You should have enough company there to keep you fed." Irony tinged her voice.

"No, really, Rebecca, I want us to get back together again. Look, I don't want to talk about it over the phone. Let's meet. I'll see you at the Clodden Spoon next to Charing Cross Road. It's close to where you live. Say yes, please?" His voice, which used to make her feel happy, only sounded like a spoiled boy who had lost his favorite toy.

"No, Cor. I've said all I wanted to say. You chose Mandy over me. She's got loads of money plus her lineage goes far enough that your other friends won't laugh at her behind her back." A sob escaped her lips, and she hated to show her emotions.

"Oh, dearest Rebecca, please let us see each other. I've broken off with Mandy. I'm going to be clean this time. I've got my job; I'm up for a promotion, it's all going well. All I need is YOU."

She became even more desperate to escape their conversation. "I'm not meeting you, Cor. I won't fall for your wishy-washy whims. We are finished."

"I'm really sorry, Rebecca. Why don't we do this? I am invited to a country weekend in Maidenhead in two weeks. It'll be fun. Let's go – let's talk there. The host is a good friend of the family. Why can't you come along, please Rebecca? I want us to make it this time." His pleading voice pulled at her emotions.

"I'll think about it. But I've got other plans today. Call me next weekend," Rebecca finally spoke, the words wrung from her throat. She hung up as he replied and then she sat back in tears.

When she gathered control of her emotions, Rebecca looked out the window where she could barely see the tall spire of Westminster outside her window. She heard noise from the traffic below, several floors down from her flat. For a few moments, she let her mind wander back to the days when she and Cor were dating. It seemed so very hard for her to imagine that those days would end up with her facing an empty future. Empty of that one person who would take care of her and assure her of a secure life.

Rebecca realized that she was still online, so she clicked on the 'send' button to let her Mother know she was okay and shut down her laptop. Neither she nor her mother, Sophia Bartholomew, liked snail mail. Rebecca wrote letters as a rule, but the distance between Connecticut and London was considerable, and she wanted to keep her parents up on her latest adventures.

It wasn't always that way. Her father, Leo Bartholomew, was the famous Heart Surgeon at Yale-New Haven Hospital. Many foreign medical institutions wooed him to come and speak at their conferences, so he was always traveling. Leo and Rebecca had a special bond that her mother Sophia supported wholeheartedly. Rebecca was Daddy's girl. This bond was a bit rocky nowadays since she and Cor had eloped.

It was a sad memory when her mother watched her leave with a suitcase in hand to elope with Cor. Rebecca avoided a showdown with her father and left her mother to cope with the fallout. Sophia had to break the news of Rebecca's elopement to Leo, who took it with no visible emotion.

It was at that moment that Rebecca heard a commotion outside her door. She felt surprised, then from the chatter outside her door, gathered that it was her next-door neighbors who came in early from their night shift. Elena, her roommate, told her about them. "They are nurses, come from Colombia, and they work the night shift." Elena, her sophisticated manner apparent in her shrug, smiled without mirth. "They always wake me up, and it's boring really."

After Cor's phone call, Rebecca forced herself to look forward to being an independent woman in London. Her instincts told her that this was not a wise decision. So many unsettling events were happening there – the terrorist attacks, the bombings, the waves of unhappy demonstrators making their voices heard about Brexit and then here she was, in the midst of it, and she felt as though she was in a dicey situation. She desperately felt alone at that instant.

As if to avoid the dire picture of her chosen place of residence – London - she flung on a jacket and slipped on boots and fled out the door.

That afternoon, hundreds of miles away, Sophia

looked up from her computer screen smiling at nobody in particular. She had just read her daughter's short email. Sophia was a beautiful brunette still, despite her being in her early fifties. A gentle expression crossed her features as she scanned Rebecca's letter.

"Oh, how good she wrote," said Sophia to nobody in particular.

Her husband, Leo, who just happened to walk in, holding in his hand a letter, heard her and asked, "Who wrote?"

"Your only child, Rebecca."

"Oh? That's nice. How is it with them?" A flinty look came to his eyes as he awaited his wife's reply.

"Well, it's not."

"Not? What do you mean?" He looked down at her and then saw she was upset. "Darling, what's happened? She alright?"

"She's broken up with Cor!"

"That's the best piece of news I've heard all week. Why are you unhappy?"

"She's decided to stay - have a job, do the London life."

He sat down in front of her and looked thoughtful. "I see."

"I guess that is her decision to make."

"Well, I have something to say about that."

"No, Leo. It's no use. Rebecca is 28 years old. She really can live on her own wherever she chooses to. She's already gone off with Cor to get married. I don't know that we can convince her to come back now."

"I want to talk to her."

"Call her you mean?"

"No. I've got an invitation from the Royal College of Surgeons. No, we are going to London. I'll be there for the lecture and conference, and then we will persuade our daughter to come back to Connecticut."

"And do what?" She raised her delicate eyebrows.

"Do her work at the hospital where she used to work. It's not a bad job. She'll get over that cad, and she's going to find somebody else."

Sophia shook her head slowly. "No, I don't think you can persuade her to come back."

"Bitten by the London bug, has she?" Leo smirked. "With all that crap the country is going through these days, I don't think she's ready to live alone there of all places. We will see about that."

"I will go with you, please." Sophia's face was sober. "I think you're right. She's in over her head living there." She paused, then asked, "Did we do the right thing with Rebecca, Leo?"

"What do you mean?"

"Well, she is our only child. She had everything she ever wanted. Rebecca got all she asked. Ralph Corcoran was the one that made her want to get married – he was a charmer, you remember?"

"Yes. I remember." Leo's lips formed a grim line. "I don't know why you want to beat us up over how we raised our daughter. So, she is our only little girl grown up. But she won't last long in London."

"I'm getting scared now, Leo."

"So am I. I think she'll have to figure out it's not the best place to live. She has NO support systems. Corcoran, even if he was an awful character – he did love her in his way."

"So, you understand that, then?"

"I think we can stay with her for a few weeks and see about getting her to see it our way," said Leo.

"When are we going?"

"Next Wednesday. The meeting is on Friday. Figure out we'll stay the week or maybe two. I'm going to let the hospital know. I need to find that new Chief Resident and tell him he's got all my cases for the time being."

Sophia glanced down at her computer and the email from her daughter. A smile crept across her lips and then she flung her arms up with a little giggle. A moment later she scrolled through the rest of her email and saw the words: **"Britain raises its terror limit to maximum levels after an attack in Manchester."**

Sophia's hand trembled involuntarily as she raised it to her cheek.

Chapter Two

The morning had stretched to half-past ten as Rebecca

got out of her building clad in black tennis shoes, grey

leggings and a long slim tee under a charcoal pea coat.

Her hair was loose around her face; a pair of sunglasses

hid her blue-green eyes from view.

The bluster of traffic wasn't too overwhelming.

Rebecca was used to that. She had been in London for

two months. Cor had left her for a wealthy widow that

promised to keep him from going into more debt. So Rebecca acted quickly to find a flat to escape from this untenable living situation he left her in.

As she strolled down Portobello Road, she felt a tremendous energy that overcame her and lifted her spirits. The memories of all the fights with Cor and the final days of their relationship faded like a soft cloud in the sunshine.

She stood outside a bookstore and decided to go in for a browse, further encouraged by the fact that the bookstore was also a coffee shop. Rebecca entered it and was immediately aware of a warm spirit that came from the place. A teenaged waiter waved at her and said, "Sit wherever you wish. I'll be by to take your order."

Rebecca sat down beside a giant wall of books, next to a window that had a box of delphinium and baby's breath on the ledge outside. The place seemed friendly enough, and several customers were already deep in their books while they munched on their food.

The boy came by and said, "Here's what we have today. Kippers, bangers and mash, toad in the hole, and some coffee. What do you like this morning?"

She tried to remember what these were and then said, "Bangers and mash and a big mug of coffee please."

"Done!" He smiled at her cheerfully and went away.

Rebecca settled back and took out her cell phone to check her messages. The sunlight streamed through the curtains and illuminated her figure as she reclined, leaning a little against the bookshelf. She was unused to being alone still. Usually, Cor was with her and amused her with his charming stories or comments. Her primary concern now was that she was eating alone, in a public restaurant, without much of a chance at meeting or seeing anyone she knew.

She did not know a significant number of people in London as of yet. All the people she had met were Cor's friends, and they all seemed to think she was odd. Being an American, and having an accent (even though she felt as though they had an accent instead of her) they tended to ignore her or not laugh at her American jokes. And then there were the few people at the hospital whom she could count with the fingers of her left hand. There was her boss, Mr. Ham, who looked at her with some amount of unease (again the American angle). The secretary of Social Work, Mrs. Roberta Bellingham - a woman who was in her fifties might be someone she could befriend. Then her coworker and peer, Marjorie Stitz – the other social worker in her late 30's, whom she had to shadow to meet her acceptance as a permanent employee.

Rebecca remembered her mother's words about whether she really ought to return to Connecticut. Her lips curled in contempt. She hated Connecticut. She didn't like the people she knew, and she felt as though everyone judged her on her appearance, her father's status and her mother's social position.

The food came finally. The waiter lingered and observed her reaction. "You're not from around here, are you?" He said.

"No. I'm - uh - from America."

"Oh."

"Yes - I came a few months ago."

"Touristing?"

"No, not really. I'm working at the Charing Cross hospital. Down the road."

"Oh," He said again. He had dirty blond hair,

pimples, and a lanky figure. He shifted his weight on the other foot. "Well, welcome, I guess. You want to live here?"

"I do." Rebecca sounded unsure. Then she repeated it firmly. "Yes, I do. I want to make a go of it. "

"Sorry to hear that." He looked sympathetically at her. "So you want to live here and be like an immigrant, is that it?"

"I do, I think so anyway." She felt flustered. "I've gotten the fiancée visa, but now I need to change that to a working visa. I'm no longer engaged, but I want to see how I can live in London."

"It shouldn't be hard. I know some people who have done that without much trouble. Good luck to you, then."

"Thanks!"

The sound of a man's voice from the back came to their ears. "Jeremy, what about some coffee for a poor starving and sleepy bloke?"

The boy stood straight and jerked his head upwards. He waved at the man. "Coming soon, Mr. Reed."

Rebecca glanced at the source of the voice and saw a tall man with light brown hair sitting down at a table close to the door. He was good-looking and familiar in some way to Rebecca. He caught her looking at him, and he gave a slight nod and a smile. Rebecca turned away quickly and addressed her cell phone with assiduous attention. She felt her cheeks warm up with a blush.

Jeremy ambled over to Mr. Reed and said, "Sorry, Mr. Reed. What can I get for you today?"

"What about some coffee and some of your eggs

and potato?"

"How d'you want your eggs?"

"Scrambled."

"Okay, will be back in a jiffy."

"Thank you."

His voice was warm, deep and had a soft English accent. The man named Reed sat back in his chair and surveyed the room. His eyes alighted on the slim figure of Rebecca by the window, and the expression on his face changed. A slight frown crossed his brow.

Rebecca tried to think of something else, but it was difficult to do. The presence of this man was creating a disturbance in her thoughts that she couldn't identify. When the food arrived, she attacked it with a ferocity that reflected her inner turmoil.

As she focused on eating her meal, she became aware of a presence next to her. She looked up guardedly and found herself staring up at a pair of blue eyes smiling down at her. Rebecca let go of her fork, and it slid down the side of her plate. "Oh, hello."

"You don't remember me, I'm guessing." Peter Reed said.

"I – I think I've met you, but I can't seem to place it." She replied truthfully, swallowing hard.

"I'm Peter Reed. I met you at Elena's flat."

Her feelings rushed up to the top of her head and then made her cheeks flush crimson. "Oh, THAT's who you are."

"I wanted to come and check on you – ah, Rebecca, right?"

"Yes. Rebecca. That's me." She heard her voice as surprisingly firm, but her legs felt like water. "Well, it's very nice to see you again, Mr. Reed."

"My friends call me Peter."

"It's nice to see you again, Peter."

"If you ever need anything, please don't hesitate to call me." He produced a calling card and placed it next to her abandoned fork.

"Thanks."

He left her side and she slunk into her chair. Rebecca smiled despite her loss of composure. It was almost like a dream to have a conversation with Peter Reed. *Peter.* His name went through her mind over and over.

Once she was finished eating, she decided not to hurry away. She wanted to share this meal with Peter Reed, despite the distance between them in the room. Rebecca was itching to share this news with her mother, but she held off and acted naturally by finishing her meal and then spending time scrolling through her Facebook app.

The waiter didn't come to give her the check yet, so she started to think why did she not wish to cross paths with Peter. Her mind circled at this question. This man was Elena's fiancé. Peter Reed. The realization made her senses swoon and then she felt sad. *Oh, my God. He's got someone* else. She felt so sorry that life had given her a lemon in Cor and that Elena, lucky girl, got the dashing Mr. Reed.

No, Rebecca, you really can't want someone else's guy, she told herself dejectedly as she made her way to the checkout counter.

"Leaving already?" Jeremy said as he took her money.

"I've finished my meal, and I have some things to do. Errands, you know."

"Ok. Hope I see you again. You ought to try the

other recipes we have."

"Sure." She smiled and pocketed her change. She didn't bother to figure out whether she got the right amount. Her money skills weren't that great with dollars and cents, and they were poorer with British money, mostly with the conversions.

She felt as though a tremendous weight lifted off her shoulders when she left the place. Rebecca walked quickly leaving the clamoring thoughts behind, thoughts that made her feel convinced that this man would have to be avoided by all means. Thankfully, Elena was not in town, and she would not return after the end of the month when Rebecca would take over the flat. *Fat chance that Peter would wander in to look for Elena,* Rebecca said to herself.

Still, her thoughts kept at her about Peter Reed. What was he doing - something in The City? How did he meet Elena? What she remembered was his quiet and yet attractive presence. The smile in his eyes as he gazed down at her was still fresh in her memory.

She shook her head as if to regain her calm.

Rebecca ran after a bus and got into it. She was breathless as she sat down on the deck level and decided to write her mother another email. The thought of running to email her Mom every time she needed to talk to someone made her feel sad – she felt friendless in this new world of London.

She hunkered down and then started to write her mother.

Dear Mom, I'm now taking a bus tour. It's a beautiful day, but it looks like rainclouds ahead. I wish you were with me. When could we see each other again? I don't want to go on vacation yet because I just started work, but I wish you would come here. Surely Daddy would let you visit for a bit. I think you can convince him

that you MUST come to London. I will have room in the

flat when my roommate quits the lease in several days."

Rebecca looked up pausing at her email. The

sights of London flew by as they passed Trafalgar

Square, then through Piccadilly Circus. She could crane

her neck to see the Shard and somewhere behind that the

Tower Bridge. The sights were so grand and gave her

heart a lift once again. She was in London. She loved it

more than she loved anything else at that moment.

The rain began to fall. Rebecca went on with her

email:

"I'm hoping to talk to someone about how Cor

and I broke up. I don't think I'm the one for someone

like him. I'd spend too much time trying to change him.

I can't talk about him now. I wonder why we ever got

engaged. What a fool I am! I feel like talking to

somebody. Do you think I ought to find a shrink? I'm not ashamed of that at all. I think plenty of these Londoners have a shrink or something. Maybe I'll ask around."

She sent her email and felt immediately better.

The rain poured down and soon flooded the streets. Rebecca sighed and tried not to dwell on the distraction that Mr. Reed gave her that morning. His coming to say "Hello" was kind of him. But she sensed a certain tautness in him. A holding back, a sort of repressed feeling or inability to say what was on his mind. His face was handsome and even charming when he smiled. When she met him before when he came to fetch Elena, his manner was the same. A tightly held emotion that, if let loose, would be like a lit fuse that would explode and cause all manner of damage. A man that held back his feelings, that were only known to him.

Not to anybody else.

Rebecca shook her head briefly to dispel the encroachment of more speculative thoughts. Did she think he was a repressed and dangerous man? She had never met an Englishman other than Cor. Cor was the opposite, charming, alive, happy, and careless. Peter Reed was capable of charm, probably not as easy to love, full of sex appeal. This stoic demeanor would be released when he was with the right person.

Sexual appeal. There, that was the idea that Rebecca had avoided thinking and it came anyway. The bus swerved sharply and several passengers gave a laughing whoop. Rebecca decided to look up Peter Reed on Google. She took up her cell phone and typed in his name.

Peter Reed. Head of Grantham Reed Investments. The City address. Single. 38 years old.

Nothing else. Another link said he played football for a while after he left university. What university? It seemed unclear. There was another less prominent link. Member of *The Union*, at Oxford. There, Rebecca smiled happily. *He's ideal*, she thought. *I'd be glad to show HIM off to my parents.*

She leaned against the window, disregarding the drip of water that came in through a leaky hole. Her face wore a happy expression. She was becoming persuaded that Peter Reed would be a darn sight better than Ralph Corcoran. Soon, the sight of Notting Hill's unique neighborhood with its curving landscape came into view and the bulk of the passengers, mainly tourists, disembarked.

Rebecca decided not to get off. She wanted to return to her flat and have a hot drink to warm up her cold body. It wasn't the real reason, she thought ruefully. *I'm falling for this guy; heaven help me.*

Chapter Three

That same morning, Peter Reed got finished with his

meal and paid his bill. He walked out into the dim

morning light as the rain steadily dropped against the

pavement. He had on a light Burberry jacket. The soft

rain pelted him without much of it disturbing his

demeanor. He neither crouched to avoid the rain nor ran

to escape it. Instead, he crossed the street leisurely to

where his Porsche was waiting. The car was black, with

tinted windows.

Just as he got inside, his cell phone buzzed. He stared at it and then decided to answer by pressing the button on his steering wheel. "Peter here."

"It's Michelle, Mr. Reed," a woman's voice came on. "Mr. Watkins wants to have a meeting with you."

"Tell him I'm on my way." He rang off, and started his car, veering it out of its parking slot and moving it into the sparse London traffic.

Peter's face was like a granite statue's - lean with hard planes. His eyes were a dark blue, with a straight nose and lips that compressed into a thin line. He wore an expressionless demeanor while his eyes darted left and right to check on oncoming traffic. The rain left small droplets of water on his hair making him look romantic.

Once he got into Mr. Watkins' office building, situated in a nondescript part of Islington, Peter went up the rickety elevator and then got off on the fifth floor. It was an ancient building, which had undergone cosmetic repairs on the facade. This building housed *Watkins, Glen, and Corrigan, Barristers-at-Law*.

The door was ajar when he got to it. He entered and saw Michelle, Mr. Watkins' secretary, standing by a file cabinet. She was pretty and fetching in her dark navy power suit. She looked up at him with puppy eyes which he ignored. "Hello, Michelle. Mr. Watkins in there?" He nodded over to the conference room.

"Hello, Mr. Reed. Yes. He's got some visitors, I'm afraid." She bit her lip as though she felt guilty for giving information.

"Fine." Peter walked past her and opened the

door to a room that was a well-appointed conference area. There was a long table, with leather-bound chairs around it, and some of them occupied by three men. The man at the head of the table looked up with a frown; then he smiled briefly.

"Peter Reed. Good of you to come so quickly – at a moment's notice."

"I was just in the neighborhood," Peter lied.

"Let me introduce you." Mr. Henderson Watkins said, turning his glance to the man next to him on his right. "This is Sir Wither Stone. Sir Wither is from the Home Office. And on my left is Captain Jack Perkins. He's from the US Counterintelligence."

"Good to meet you both." Peter remained standing but sat down when Watkins motioned him to.

Captain Perkins was a well-built man, of about 48 years of age. His face had a smattering of freckles.

He wore the costume of a businessman: a navy striped suit. Sir Wither was much older, in his sixties. His face was long and pale except for a red tinge to his nose. He wore dark navy as well. A Malacca cane hung on the arm of his chair.

Mr. Watkins was about the same age as Sir Wither but looked stout. A pipe was perched by his elbow which he puffed at from time to time. He wore a grey suit with a fuchsia handkerchief discretely folded within his breast pocket.

"I've been visited by Sir Withers and Mr. Perkins on the topic of the spate of terrorist attacks in the City and other parts of England. Mr. Reed is our agent under cover. We hope — at least, MI5 hopes, which Mr. Reed's assignment will help to neutralize the source of these attacks."

All eyes were on Peter who added nothing but

remained silent.

"I am happy to know that MI5 is in this case as I am sure everyone assumes," Sir Wither spoke with a condescending tone.

"Obviously, Sir Wither," Watkins said evenly. "Now, we all know - well, Peter does now — that while those who perpetrated these attacks have been taken into custody or neutralized, the origin of these stratagems is still at large. He or She - I try to keep within the PC culture," He smiled at his comment, "may be blithely going in and out of the country, finding more money and sources of power to get the British Isles in a terror watch the likes of which we have not seen since the last War."

"I'm going to put in what we know," The CIA man spoke. "This originator, if you can call that person, appears to be alive and well on the outskirts of London. Somewhere in Maidenhead."

"That is congruent with my sources," Peter said.

Perkins raised his eyebrows. "You know this? How could you? We only just found out this morning."

"I think Mr. Reed is a bounty of knowledge," Watkins said.

"What else do you know, Mr. Reed?" Sir Withers asked, with more respect in his demeanor.

Peter replied, "I am not at liberty to divulge. I don't wish to give you all in case we are not alone in this room." He stopped. Peter glanced at Perkins with some caution. Watkins and Peter avoided each other's glances.

"I'm sorry," Perkins was becoming red-faced. "We are supposed to be united in this war against terror. Yet, you don't wish to divulge?"

Reed looked at him with a hard glance. "I do not. I don't know much about you, and the CIA has been falling on their job as of late. You are likely someone who was sent to find out and that I am not in any mood to go along with it. I haven't met Sir Wither before today, and so I feel no compunction to tell him anything either."

Sir Wither looked dismayed. "Mr. Reed, this is highly disagreeable. Mr. Watkins, how do we keep up with making a team when Mr. Reed won't play?"

Watkins sat back and steepled his fingers. "Let's say we have met. I am asking Mr. Reed to report only to me now. It is my place to apprise you both of anything that — "

"This is preposterous." Perkins stood up and started to head towards the door.

"Sit down, Mr. Perkins," Watkins spoke with a steely undertone to his voice.

"I refuse to. I am a loyal soldier of the United States of America, went to the best military academy, and served two long tours in Afghanistan. I want to serve the city of London and help the citizens to get rid of this terrorist scourge. What more do you want to know? I am —"

"What you are saying is that you need information that isn't really going to help at this time," interrupted Peter with a silken voice. "You all only need to know that I know where this originator is at the moment. I am not going to endanger my operation nor my operatives by telling more. Is that clear?"

He stood up and walked out the door. The outburst from Peter made them slump in their seats.

"What the hell did we do this meeting for, then?" demanded Perkins.

"It was a waste of time, wasn't it?" Watkins smiled almost with a sweetness that belied the sharpness of his expression.

"Yes, it is." Sir Wither stood up taking his cane with him. "I have to go — another meeting, you know."

"CIA and MI5 have an agreement to share information," Perkins said morosely.

"Don't worry. When we have more we can divulge, we will let you know," replied Watkins.

"Where did you find this Reed person anyway?" demanded Perkins.

Sir Wither paused at this, changed his mind, and then resumed his journey to the open door. He heard the short reply from Watkins, but he ignored it.

"It's classified," Watkins replied.

"We can find out about Reed."

"It will be all a pack of lies. You should know that, Perkins. Now, why don't you let things go for now? I wouldn't bother about Reed. He comes highly recommended. We ought to be more focused on the matter at hand. Let's not pick on each other when we have the safety of the country at hand. I will, if you want to feel better, reprimand Peter later and ask him to be more civil should we meet again. I appreciate you wanting to know more, but you should know that the fewer people who know, the safer the operation is."

Perkins shrugged his shoulders. "I guess." He stiffened his back then said, "Yes, ok. Fine. You know where to reach me."

Sir Withers and Major Perkins left right after the exchange and said nothing to anybody as they walked out. As the door closed behind them, Peter emerged from behind the tall armoire and went back into the conference room.

Watkins was filling his pipe and saw Peter. "Oh, I thought you'd left for good."

"No. I wanted to tell you that I don't trust that

Perkins. I've been given information that he is playing both sides against the middle."

"I see." Watkins looked unsurprised. "If that's the case, I'm glad we didn't say anything important." His eyes widened at Peter who sat lounging beside the table. "You're looking as though you want to say more. What is it this time, Peter? Is the liaison with Elena Ramos making you unhappy?"

"N-No."

"What is it, good grief, tell me. I haven't got all day."

"She's rooming with an American girl, the name of Rebecca Bartholomew. I can't tell yet if she's clean or not. Being an American these days, one cannot be sure of their sympathies."

"Oh. I'll ask Moorehead to send you a file on the American girl presently."

"I saw her today. At a breakfast shop."

"She is a tourist maybe? Is she staying for a few months? I don't see why you care, Reed."

"I think she needs to get out of this situation with Elena."

"Are you saying Elena is going to recruit her?"

"Possibly."

"Hell."

"Exactly my thoughts."

"Is she that gullible looking?"

"She's like all the tourists – all goggle-eyed, full of idealism, lots of money probably, and no real friends in this godforsaken city."

"Don't worry too much about this girl. I think perhaps you are attracted?" Watkins slanted a glance at him. Peter's silence gave him away. Watkins pursed his lips. "I'd say you need to find a way to ignore this attraction, Peter. We can't have anybody gum up the operation. Nobody. Do you understand?"

Peter's expression looked almost defenseless.

"Peter Reed, you have to stop what you look like you want to do."

"Shut up." Peter got up and paced the room. "I've never had this happen. What happened to me? I have Elena eating out of my hand. She's supposed to be my fiancée. I now have to deal with this American girl who makes it hard for me to think straight."

"Oh dear." Watkins rolled his eyes upward. "I might have to transfer you, old chap. You can't do this operation like this."

Peter stopped pacing and went to him. "NO."

"I will say this. If you ever make a mistake and follow your baser feelings, that will mean a few dozen operatives' lives will be at stake. We'd have to do a lot of cleaning up, get them transferred out and give good alibis for it. Do you see my point yet?"

"I will make it a point to have the girl leave the country."

Watkins looked at him with doubt in his eyes. "I'm sure she'll like being bundled up into a bag and sent via Royal Mail overseas. How the devil will you do it?"

"I don't know," Peter said crossly. "I do NOT know."

They were silent. Peter looked at Watkins and said quietly. "Let me have a few days. I'll let you know if I need to be taken out of the operation."

Reed's words gave Watkins' a tight feeling in the chest. He said, "I will give you until the weekend. Should you choose to pursue this girl, I will have to ask for your resignation and your weapon."

"Fine."

Chapter Four

When Peter arrived at his posh residence in Notting Hill,

a short burst of beeps was erupting from his telephone.

Peter closed the door and strode to where his telephone

sat. He read the caller ID and picked up the phone.

"Peter Reed." He spoke crisply into the receiver.

"It's Rodney's Pub calling. We wanted to check

with you whether you are still requiring a case of wine or

some other type of liquor for next month's

subscription?"

"Sure. I need you to deliver me a case of Glenfiddich. How about in about 20 minutes?"

"Right." The man rang off.

Peter took off his jacket and took a seat next to his desk. His flat was sparsely decorated. His only luxury seemed to be a long leather divan that occupied the middle of the living room, and a vintage mahogany desk. There were letters that were unopened and he sorted through them and tossed most of them into the small round trash container that sat on the floor next to the desk. His face looked stormy, as though he was still working out a difficult problem.

Within the twenty minutes, the doorbell rang from downstairs. Without asking, Peter buzzed the visitor in. From the video of the entrance, he could see the man carrying a box. The man appeared at his door with a smile, wearing a Macintosh jacket. "Lots of Glenfiddich, my lord Reed." He said in a singing voice.

"Hell, don't broadcast it, Moorhead," Peter said laconically. He opened the door wide and let the man inside.

Moorhead was a sandy-haired, freckle-faced man in his twenties. His face was adorned with spectacles that made him look years older.

Peter looked at Moorhead closely. "Are you growing a beard, old boy?"

"No, I've just been up all night."

"Oh."

Moorhead flushed. "At the office, Peter."

"Of course." Peter grinned.

"Where does the case go?"

"Same place. Just put it there and I'll get to it."

"Operations wants to know if you want to send them anything."

"No." Peter stood by the window and peered out the curtains.

"No, not parked illegally," Moorhead said, anticipating Reed's anxiety about his people attracting attention.

"Fine." Peter came to the desk and sat on its edge. His face looked expectantly at Moorhead. "What do you know?"

"Elena's having a big weekend party in a fortnight. Are you going?"

"She hasn't told me."

"Really? But you're, like — together."

"Well, she hasn't told me," Peter remarked easily.

Moorhead looked at him doubtfully but went on, "She is inviting various characters that we have been thinking of putting on our watch." He paused, and then said, "She's holding the party at Max Revenor's mansion, you know."

Peter laughed. "Is that right? I understand why she might not want to invite me, then."

"Max Revenor's the one we want, and he's known to have his own particular set of hoods that keep him out of arm's length. You DO know that Elena's close to him?"

"I do. That's why I have to pretend she's my fiancée."

Moorhead flushed again. "I wanted you to know that there's one particular person that she has asked the weekend party. Someone named Rebecca Bartholomew."

"Who's that?"

"Elena's roommate."

"Oh." Peter's face clouded. Then his face cleared and he recalled the brunette at the coffee shop this morning. "I remember her. Yes. Pretty - a bit naive — American, right?"

"Yes. Rebecca's a lovely lass. Totally unsuited to come to these shindigs. I really must tell you the weekend party is NOT as it might seem to the ordinary observer."

"Yes, I know. Well, I can't do anything about this Rebecca woman."

"She's the ex of this medico who's deep into the gambling stuff. Name of Ralph Corcoran. He's going there too, by the way. Elena's friend. Lots of bad eggs there."

"Why do you care about this Bartholomew girl?" Reed asked in an off-hand way.

"I don't. But it's going to look bad if our

operation got out of hand. And that this girl will be in the way if you get my meaning." Moorhead plunged on. "She's an American, my dear Peter. It's going to set off Whitehall. I can't bear to think those American CIA men swarming all over us when someone from their country is a casualty of a terror plot!"

"Yes, I do get your meaning. No, our operation won't get out of hand. I will check on this Bartholomew girl and find a way to get her not to come."

Moorhead chuckled. "I'd like to know how you can prevent that from happening."

"I'm good at getting in the way of people's plans, remember?" Peter said with a devilish grin.

"Let's hope so." Moorhead persisted. "She has a rather important father in the States. Could get sticky if — "

"If that's all, then let's give you something for

the Glenfiddich," Peter said dismissively. He took out his wallet and pulled out a few bills. He gave them to Moorhead who pocketed the money.

"You know to keep this information to yourself, Moorhead. Go down the back way and get out without being noticed."

"As per protocol. Okay, fine." Moorhead headed for the back and disappeared behind the door.

#

Chapter Five

Peter stretched his lean body and yawned. He came around to the kitchen and opened the box of Glenfiddich. Inside were two bottles of the scotch and a sheaf of folders. He took the Glenfiddich out and set them on his countertop. The folders took him some time to dislodge from the box, but finally, he began to examine their contents. He took time to read them and then he took them to the incinerator and lit a match to one of the folders. He shut the incinerator close and then went to his bedroom where he changed into his evening clothes.

There was a message on his telephone that had escaped his notice. He flipped the switch and heard a woman's voice. Velvet-sound and laden with years of smoking. "Peter darling, this is Elena. I'm afraid I have to cancel our dinner tonight. Something's just come up, and I can't leave it. Please forgive me, dear Peter. I'll call you tomorrow. Kiss kiss."

Peter's face revealed nothing of his disappointment if any. Elena's last-minute cancellation didn't seem to bother him at all.

Elena Ramos put down the phone and reached for a cigarette. Her olive skin glowed as the fire of her lighter illuminated her face. She wore no obvious

makeup, but her lipstick was intact and delineated her

pouty lips. She had dark hair and brown eyes, and there

was a very distinct manner to her that betrayed a life of

greed and ambition. She wore several necklaces, and her

diamond ring flashed on her hand - given to her by Peter

- which spoke of her success in getting one of the most

eligible bachelors in England.

"Too bad he's not home." She breathed the

smoke from the cigarette. Her voice was like velvet,

mainly due to years of smoking and drinking good wine.

"I'd not worry much about it. Peter's rather

good at taking disappointment." The man sitting at the

divan sounded uninterested. "He's always on the go,

anyway. Stands to reason he'd cancel more like than you

would?"

"Yes," she replied. "But I think he'd have

wanted more than a moment's notice."

"Stop fretting, Elena. I am sure he will forgive you." His tone was meaningful as his eyes, dark and malicious, gazed up at her. "We have more important things to discuss."

"We could have put it off for another evening, Max."

"No," Max said with a hint of brusqueness. "I want us to discuss the party we intend to hold in a fortnight."

"Oh alright." She sat back and gave him her full attention. "What do we still need to do?"

"Did you discuss the shipment with Brussels?"

"I did. They are shits. I told them to pay me by the usual means and they sent the money to my real account."

"Elena," Max said wearily. "When will you learn?"

"I know it's my fault but - I cannot undo it now."

"What if the authorities find out? They will see this account and the depositors business name."

"The business is legitimate."

"It's a front for God's sake, Elena. I HATE this." He got up and paced the floor. "I want you to - DAMN it, I want you to take care of it."

"Look, my love," Elena leaned over pleadingly. "Brussels IS legitimate and I do their LEGITIMATE business for them. There is NO reason to feel worried."

"You will be made to answer for this if this operation we will have in two weeks time will be a failure." Max's eyes were sharp. "Elena, tonight I will not let you in my bed. I have lost my taste for your delicious talents."

Elena looked at him as though she were regarding a churlish and spoiled boy. "I will not be leaving until tomorrow. I've already settled my things here."

"We cannot discuss it now. Come back later - maybe after an hour. I will have had time to unwind."

Elena smiled alluringly. "I know how to make you feel unwound."

Max glanced at her sleepily. "Let me think about it. I want you to go to your room."

Her smile brightened. "Of course, Max." She got up and passed him on the way to the door.

Max sighed and then when he was alone, he reached into his pocket and took out his cell phone. He punched a number and then listened. "I want to talk to

Perkins."

He waited and then when the voice came on, he said, "I'm almost ready for the party." He paused. "Oh, really. So, he knows about me? Well, we have a few things prepared for Mr. Reed." He listened to the laughter on the other line. Then he said, "Thanks, Jack. See you soon."

Chapter Six

Rebecca found her mail sitting on the floor by her door as she walked to her flat. It was not all that interesting to her, except for a note that looked familiar in its writing. "Cor." She said in dismay. Rebecca tossed the note card aside and put the key into its slot.

She unlocked her door, pushed it aside, then slammed it shut. It was all she could do to express her unhappiness. The day out in the city was rainy, mud and mixtures of splashed water ruined her leggings. She wanted to get out of her clothes and sit in a hot bath.

Her mouth made a moue as she considered the note from Cor. She had about enough of his constant letters and cards. The phone calls were interminable.

She made a fire in the grate and then pulled off all her clothes. She walked naked to the bathroom and turned on the tap. Rebecca put some bath gel in the collecting water in the tub and then wandered to her room to find a robe and a magazine to read.

She went to the kitchen, slinging on the robe and belting it, and searched for glass and a bottle of wine. Rebecca hummed to herself. "Time to relax!" She said to herself.

Once the wine had filled her glass, Rebecca walked to the bathroom. She was about to get into the tub when the doorbell rang.

"Damn." She tried to ignore it. The doorbell sounded again, with insistent beeps.

Rebecca wondered if it was Elena, without her key again. "Hold on!"

She put her robe on again and then half-tripped to the door. She opened the door saying, "I really don't like it when you can't keep track of your keys, Elena —"

"No, sorry. Wrong person."

The man at the door was Peter Reed. He looked taller and more frightening to her. She saw the look in his eyes and instinctively clutched her robe closer to her neck.

He saw her movement and then smiled. It was a disarming smile. Almost delighted. "Hell, I'm not as bad as that. I'd like to come in, please."

"Well, Elena's not here." She protested, trying to block his way and failing miserably.

"Oh, I know she's decided to hide in her bedroom?"

"No, she is NOT here. I told you that."

"Let me try to prove you wrong." Peter strode into the second bedroom and opened the door.

An empty room gaped at them both.

"Hell, that's not good." He looked puzzled and then went back to where Rebecca stood.

"Where is she?"

"I don't know." Rebecca was fast losing her temper. Her bath beckoned to her. The wine, the steamy water with lots of bubbles and suds.

"I'm supposed to have met her for dinner."

"No, I don't have a clue. Please leave."

"Ok, I will leave." He looked at her again before he stepped away. "It was nice to see you the other day at the coffee shop."

"Yes, very nice to have met you."

"I think you need to leave. I've had a long day, and I need to have some peace."

"You have a charming American accent. Where do you come from in America?"

She put her lips firmly together and crossed her arms.

He laughed and then as though by impulse, he chucked her on the chin. "You're a corker, my dear Rebecca. What's your last name?"

"Bartholomew." She barely spoke. Her alarm bells were at high volume in her head. She was talking to a very attractive man, and she was only in her bathrobe.

"Nice to meet you. Let's have some lunch sometime. Would you like to have lunch with me?"

"No. Now, please leave."

He held up his hands and then stepped backward till he got to the door whereupon he turned and closed it behind him.

Chapter Seven

Rebecca walked into the office clad in her comfortable but elegant linen dress that flowed slightly outwards as she walked, a beige colored dress and her yellow cotton cardigan sweater loose about her shoulders. She found Mrs. Bellingham on the phone and her colleague Marjorie Stitz typing at her desk. Neither one looked up to say hello, as both seemed to have gotten into a trance of work.

Rebecca took her place at her desk, which was closest to the coffee machine. She sat down, put her bag in a drawer and logged into her computer. The door to her boss' office was half ajar, and Rebecca could hear voices inside. She tried not to listen and checked her emails.

Nothing important, she decided, and so she got her coffee mug out and poured herself a cup. "How were your weekends, Mrs. Bellingham? Marjorie?" She said in a conversational tone.

"Huh." Muttered Mrs. Bellingham, as she hung up the phone. "Mr. Sturgeon is not happy that we haven't checked in with his patient. Rebecca, why don't you follow up on that? I hear he's to be discharged today sometime. We need to make sure the patient isn't going to ignore therapist recommendations, seeing as how he's suffered a breakdown."

"Musn't do that." Marjorie agreed, looking up from her laptop. She had a pair of glasses, horn-rimmed, her reddish hair all askew as she was wont to drag her fingers through it periodically. Her chin was prominent and gave an appearance to her face as something like the crescent moon, except that she had green eyes. Mandy smiled. "I had a good weekend. How was yours?"

"Oh, it was good, as far as it went." She chuckled. "I think I'll go and check on the patient now. Do you remember the name, Mrs. Bellingham?"

"Oh, let me find it." Mrs. Bellingham ruffled through her files. "Ah yes, Mahmood Indi."

"Ok, how about the room number?"

"Room C-345. It's in the psych ward."

Marjorie gave her shoulders a shivering movement. "I'm sorry but that spooks me still having been here for five years now."

"Don't prejudice the girl, Marjorie," Mrs. Bellingham said with a frown.

Then, Rebecca's telephone rang. "Rebecca Bartholomew here." Rebecca stood by her desk, rifling through her things for pen and notepad.

"Hi, Sweetheart." The voice came on and gave her a jolt.

"Hi, Cor."

"Listen, I am hoping against hope to see you for lunch today. Or even a coffee. Is it ok to meet someplace? I want to talk."

"I'm sorry Cor, I am very busy today. I told you we are finished."

"I can't accept that, my love. I want us to reconcile. Please say yes. I'll be good, I promise."

Rebecca's lips were a thin line of annoyance. "No, Cor. It's over between us."

"Look, I've got that invitation to a country weekend party. It's up by Maidenhead. You really might like it. You and I could come - no strings, mind. I'll be your perfect escort."

Something in the words he said made Rebecca's head lift in reaction. "Maidenhead?" She remembered that was where Elena Ramos was living when she wasn't in London.

"Yes. You know they have a lovely house - the Revenors. Family friends and all that sort of thing. I want you to come with me. It will be loads of fun. The family's been in the peerage for centuries."

Rebecca paused, and then said, "No, I am not interested, Cor. I think you should find yourself somebody else to take with you."

She hung up and then announced, "I'll be off to Mr. Indi's room."

"Good luck," Marjorie said with an ironic wave of her hand.

As Rebecca left, the door to Mr. Ham's office opened wide, and two men came out. "Sorry, Mr. Reed, we really can't allow you to talk to our patients. You've already had that message from the Hospital Administrator - they are not to be interrogated."

"I don't see why not. I've had no issues before." Peter Reed stood tall and looked askance at Mr. Ham, who was a foot shorter and twice as wide.

"It's something to do with Mr. Indi's being in the psychiatric ward. Too much pressure will likely set him off. We will have to say no to your request, Mr. Reed. Really you must let this go."

Peter looked at him with a frown and then, he

relaxed, saying, "I'm sure we'll find some way to get to him. I'll have the legal department talk to yours. I must talk to Indi, it's important."

"We can't comment."

"When is he to be released?"

"Sometime in the next 24 hours." Mr. Ham looked at Reed with a worried look. "It's all I can say. Please leave."

Peter turned and left the room, and the two women gaped at Mr. Ham. "What was THAT all about?" Asked Mrs. Bellingham.

"Oh, some sort of security thing. The man insists on interviewing Indi."

"On what grounds?" Said Mandy.

"I think on the grounds that he's Muslim and might be linked to some terrorist group." Mr. Ham threw up his hands and went back into his office, closing his door with a snap.

"Oh, my!" Mrs. Bellingham commented before she went back to her work.

As the day went on, Rebecca began to feel an encroaching feeling of dread. She had gone to visit Mr. Indi's room but he wasn't there. There were several strange men who loitered outside his room whose presence gave her a feeling of discomfort. These were Muslim men, and as she wasn't used to their type, their stares made her feel uncomfortable. She decided to head to the ward's reception area and inquired as to Mr. Indi's whereabouts.

The ward secretary looked at his file and said, "He's going through an MRI."

"MRI?" Asked Rebecca. "But he's due to be

released today. Is that normal? It would delay his discharge."

The secretary gave her a bold stare. "I don't know why you would care. Are you some sort of medical expert or nurse?"

"No, I'm from the Social Work department."

"Ha." The secretary smiled with a triumphant gleam. "It's not for me to say why he's having an MRI. Why don't you check on him again later? Or call here first." She turned away and left Rebecca feeling disappointed.

She hated having to return to the man's room. Finally, she decided to take a detour to the cafeteria and find something to soothe her psyche. She remembered her mother telling her that a little sweet would make her feel better. Rebecca felt nostalgic, but her thoughts had gotten so scattered after the call from Cor, and then not finding Indi in his room. The ward secretary's mendacity made her flee all the more to the call of the sweet cake shop in the hospital.

Her salvation, a large tea cake, and a cup of tea made her feel better. Her cell phone buzzed, and she saw the message came from Elena: "Let's meet for lunch, Rebecca. I'd like to ask you to a house party."

Another house party? Rebecca shut her cell phone down and pocketed it. It was most likely the same party that Cor mentioned to her, she thought with a frown before tackling her sweet cake.

"This is Dr. Chillingworth's office. What can I do for you?" The receptionist's voice was pleasant and smooth.

"I'm Rebecca Bartholomew. I'd like to come for a consultation, please."

"Of course. Have you been referred to by someone in the NHS?"

"No, I haven't."

"Well, then you will need to arrange for your payment at the time of service."

"That's fine," Rebecca replied. "How much?"

The receptionist told her, and Rebecca felt taken aback by the amount stated. "She has a cancellation today at three in the afternoon. Can you make it?"

"Yes, I can."

"See you then," the woman rang off.

Rebecca's phone call was not done in private. From the wings, Peter Reed watched her bright head as she made the call. He was passing by when he saw Rebecca sitting with her tea cake and tea. The look on Rebecca's face made him pause, and then he decided to listen to her call.

"Hello, there." He said after she pocketed her cell phone.

She turned her head and saw him. "Oh, hello."

"Do you work here?"

"Yes, I'm a social worker. What are YOU doing here?"

"I - I had an appointment to talk to one of the patients. May I join you?"

She reddened but allowed him to sit down. "Is that a good cake there you've got?"

"Yes. It is. Would you like some?" Good manners propelled her to share her meal.

"No, thank you," Peter replied. "I wanted to see

this patient - but the hospital won't let me see him. Is this a new policy?"

"I don't know. I am a new employee here, but I think with all the terrorist activities, people here are shy of letting anyone - a stranger - come to visit their patients. Policy, I suppose."

"Okay. I see."

"Are you someone who has authority to see people?"

"No, but I work for a solicitor. I do the legwork for him."

She looked at him skeptically. She remembered he worked in an investment firm from her Google search. Rebecca looked at him again with a guarded look. "You do the legwork?" Rebecca asked. "You look more the type who would order somebody to do your legwork for you."

Peter lifted his hand to smooth his hair in a reflex. "You're frank, Miss Bartholomew."

"No, I'm not. I'm just observant," she said in reply.

"Well, if you are, don't show it off."

"You're a guess yourself."

"Well, if you wish to get to know me, we could go for a meal sometime. How about dinner tomorrow at seven?"

Her eyes widened. "Does Elena know about how you ask any other girl out for a date?"

"Elena and I have an agreement. She goes her way, and I go mine."

"Is that how things are like in this country? Engaged people going off and having dates with men and women they aren't bound to?"

"Oh, yes, it is, actually." He lied. A smile

played on his lips. "Would you like to have a free meal, with no strings, with me tomorrow night?"

Rebecca felt the flutter in her stomach as his eyes held hers. After a small pause, she replied, "Fine. I'd like that." She dreaded Elena's reaction if she ever heard of this date.

"Ok. Good. I'll pick you up at six thirty."

"Why don't we meet there instead?"

"I'll pick you up." He insisted and then got up and left.

#

Chapter Eight

The psychologist's office was a very well appointed one. Large and comfortable chairs and lots of cushions with soft red carpeting and Wedgwood blue rugs, and the paintings on the far wall behind Dr. Chillingworth was probably an original by Ackroyd.

The chair where Dr. Lucinda Chillingworth sat was a Queen Anne chair, with the wings, pale blue with deep blue ribs that delineated the curves of the chair. A small fireplace stood by the rear wall.

Rebecca sat waiting until the doctor spoke. She looked around with interest and decided that the fee was largely due to the location of the office (Harley Street) and the appointments in her office. As well as, she mused, the educational attributes of the psychologist.

A wall plaque that emblazoned Oxford University occupied the near wall by Rebecca.

"Why are you here? Tell me about yourself." Dr. Chillingworth started the conversation. "Mind you, we have an hour so you can be expansive as you wish."

"Well, I'm from Connecticut, in the United States. I lived there and worked there in the hospital in New Haven for about three years out of college, then I met a doctor - he's from England - and we fell in love."

"Oh, I see, are you getting married then?"

"No. He turned out to be the worst choice. He

gambles. Races, cards, roulette. The whole thing. I knew he was something like that, but I felt that I could maybe distract him - make him want to do things with me and forget about all that. But he's really hardcore about it, and he's lost a fortune. His parents are rich, and they live in California. The father is in the entertainment industry. So Cor - that's his nickname - Ralph Corcoran - Cor, well, he thinks he can keep throwing money away forever."

"And you - are you then separated?"

"Yes, I've told him the wedding is off."

"Does he still try to pursue you?"

"Yes. I try to tell him to give it up."

"Do you not have any feelings for him at all then?"

"No. I hate him now. I don't want him to bother me again."

"What about going back to Connecticut?"

"I think I'd like to stay here. I have a visa to work here, and so I want to try to see how it is to live in London."

"I see." Lucinda Chillingworth pursed her lips and turned the page of her notebook. "What about your work situation? Are you happy there?"

"I am. Well, I think it's great. I enjoy the work as always. I'm a social worker."

"Good. We need more of your people to work in it. What about other things? Do you think you can find somebody new? Is that going to be a problem maybe?"

"No, well, sort of." Rebecca took a deep breath. "I met a man - he's engaged to my roommate. I've become - well I sort of have a crush on him."

The eyes of Dr, Chillingworth widened. "You are rather fast at this, aren't you?"

"No, I - I only said I have a crush on the man. I don't intend to pursue him." Rebecca said with an innocent face.

"Ok." The doctor wrote in the notebook and was silent for a while. "Have you had other romantic relationships?"

"Well, high school romances. Nothing serious."

"What about your parents?"

"My father's a surgeon. My mother's a stay at home. She's more of a social person."

"Any other siblings?"

"No," admitted Rebecca.

"What about your relationship with other people? Do you make friends easily?"

"I do. I feel glad that I live here and get to know the life in London."

Lucinda Chillingworth stopped writing. "What is

it then that you feel you want me to help you with?"

"I'm not sure. I need to talk to someone,I guess. I am new here. I feel like my relationships with men might be something we could discuss. Or at least how not to attract the wrong one again."

The doctor wrote in her notebook. Then she snapped it shut. "We're out of time. Let's make another appointment, shall we? How do three weeks sound to you?"

"Good."

"In the meantime, why don't you write in a journal so you and I can discuss whatever issues you might come upon. We can try to see where it is that is making you go into the wrong type of relationships. Goodbye."

Rebecca walked out into Harley Street dejectedly. She felt as though the doctor was angry at her for some reason. *I wonder why she hates me*, Rebecca asked herself. She decided to hail a cab to her flat and sat back in the passenger seat to think of nothing at all.

Chapter Nine

Max Revenor's phone rang later that evening as he sat in his study. A large fire blazed across from him and warmed his feet which were encased in red velvet slippers. His face was heavy and quite florid. Revenor's eyes were heavy lidded, with dark gray eyes, and his nose was long in the English way. His lips were full but not overly sensuous.

Max wore a dressing gown and a pair of reading

glasses sat on his nose. His body was not as heavy as expected like his face but was actually fit, with sinewy strength. This was his proud achievement which made many women like Elena fall like ninepins in his presence.

Without taking his eyes from the newspaper he was reading, he lifted the telephone off its cradle and spoke into the receiver. "Hello."

"Max, this is Lucinda."

"Hello, Lucy. How are you? Rather a surprise to hear from you. I hope everything's alright?"

"Oh, I'm fine, dear Max." The voice was light and flirtatious. "I wanted to tell you I'm not able to come to your house party. I've got plans to go on a trip to Bristol for a conference."

"You shrink types, my dear. Oh alright then, you have a good time. Thank you for letting me know."

"I also wanted to alert you to a person I saw in my office. Someone who you might be interested in."

"Who is that?" Max's eyes lifted their gaze to the fireplace.

"She's an American. Her name is Rebecca Bartholomew."

"Oh, and what about this Rebecca?"

"She's Ralph Corcoran's ex-fiancee. You remember the Corcoran's, don't you?"

"I do. So she was his girl was she? And she's still in town?"

"She is. Wants to stay and be part of the London scene. I thought you'd like to know."

"I don't know why I should, dear Lucy."

"Well, I think she could possibly be good to know - being alone in London, not having any friends."

There was a pause and Max frowned. "Lucy, I

don't want to meet some American girl in search of romance or more serious things. I'm past all that. Really I am."

Lucy laughed. "Sure, Max. Well, I'll just let this sit in your court."

"I am gratified you thought of me as someone who could be a paramour of this Bartholomew girl. Is she a young one?"

"She's in her twenties. Blonde and full of life. You'd love her, Max."

"I still wonder why you're telling me about her, Lucy."

"Max, I think you once told me you were looking for friends who could keep you amused."

"Oh, that." Max frowned once again. "No, I'm not looking now. I've found someone I much prefer."

"Who's that?"

"Damn your impertinence. It's a secret. Now let me alone, Lucy. Enjoy your trip." He hung up and sat back, his lips working in a fury. "Damn the woman; she's a silly matchmaker." He said to himself.

Elena entered his study, bearing a pair of glasses of wine. "Who's a silly matchmaker, Max?" She inquired.

"Oh, this psychiatrist I've seen." He replied in a gruff voice. His face relaxed into a smile as he accepted a glass of wine. "Thank you, my dear Elena. Very sweet of your to bring me something to relax."

"Was this psychiatrist trying to match you up with another woman?" Elena's smile was wary as she regarded him.

"Oh, she talked about some American girl who came to see her for a consultation. Nothing for you to worry.. I'm done with twenty-year-olds."

Elena's face had an arrested look. Then she relaxed and snuggled against his side. "Oh, my goodness. I think American girls that age are much too naive for your liking, Max."

They sat silent, sipping their wine. Max looked at the fire once again, and an image of a blonde, buxom American girl danced in the flames in the fireplace in front of him.

Chapter Ten

In the back office of 10-19 Hampstead Road sat two

people: Robert Moorehead and Margo Huxley. Both are

busy with their laptops and barely speak to each other.

A solitary overhead lamp lit the room. Their quarters

was a narrow one, just a long wooden table and the rest

of it were cupboards, and a farmhouse sized sink. The

coffee pot and teapot sat side by side on the end of the

bench that housed an old oven, and the opposite side had

one swing out grey file cabinet.

"Mmm." Spoke Moorhead and he leaned back scratching his chin.

"What's that?" Margo asked, her sleek dark hair falling over her face.

"The house party - I think we might be in for a lot of shock getting past their security - a lot of shock. The fence is electrified. There's also a passel of hounds that he keeps to make sure burglars get caught.

"So what do we do? Can't we get in with the invitees?"

"We are part of the invitees, courtesy of one of the guests. There are tons going to be there that weekend, and we will merely be one of the young and happy couples going there for the experience. Note," Moorhead held up a finger. "They are charging us a hundred quid per person to be part of the scene!"

"Then what's your worry? We are in, and so we don't need to sneak in."

"We need to sneak out, that's why. We go in; then we merge with the crowd, then when we all go our separate couple ways, that's when we do our dirty doings and put in the bugs in the house."

Margo looked up at his face with worry in her eyes. "Look, Bobby, I'm not keen on sneaking out."

"There's also the fact that the man has handlers who will be on watch whenever anyone makes an early departure."

"Ugh."

"Yes, ugh."

"Well, what about if we - " She went over to his laptop and saw that he was looking at the terrain of Revenor's estate. "Here's a thought. What if we went through the woods behind the house and kept a car somewhere beyond?"

"Good thought. But we might be followed by those damned hounds."

"I'd feed them some poisoned meat, Bobby."

"You cruel, cruel girl." Moorehead looked at her with a smile. "I think that might work but who's going to do that? Do you volunteer?"

She shrank back in disgust. "NO."

"You're MI5 now, Missy. No shrinking from the work at hand."

Margo sat down at his side. "I'm going to pretend that I have bad news from a dear aunt or something, and plead leaving early. Surely they won't ask too many questions?

"True, that might work."

The door opened, and a momentary gust of noise

from the outside bar area swept into the room. The couple looked up and saw Peter enter. "How goes it, team?"

"We're figuring out logistics," Moorhead said.

"Good. I'll leave you both to that. I'm here to say I've made contact with Miss Bartholomew."

Margo looked interested. "Oh, how did that go?"

"We have a date tomorrow night."

Moorhead gave him a warning look. "You need to know that some quarters are interested in Miss Bartholomew."

"Oh?"

"Yes. I've been told by our listeners that she consulted a psychiatrist and the same psychiatrist is a BIG friend of Max Revenor."

"I see." Peter sat on the edge of the table. "What more, Moorhead?"

"It also seems that Miss Bartholomew has confessed to being more than attracted to YOU."

"Good." Peter smiled briefly. "I'm sure I can help her along with that."

"Really, Peter," Margo said with a hint of admiration in her voice. "You are the quintessential MI5 agent. A girl in every - er - "

"Never you mind," Peter said coldly.

Chapter Eleven

Rebecca sat mute next to Peter as they drove out of the parking space next to the restaurant they just left. Dinner was an eternity for her as it was only the first time he had spent more than five minutes with her. Peter, dressed in a dark navy jacket and trousers, and a crisp white shirt showing off the tanned skin of his neck made her feel conscious, and she was mad at herself for being tongue tied almost all through the dinner. They ordered the same thing - lobster bisque, linguine and clams with butter and parsley, and a dessert of tiramisu. The wine was poured liberally for Peter who seemed not the least affected by it.

He sat across from her looking at her with a half-smile, as though he knew something about her that she didn't know, or, didn't want him to know.

Finally, she laid down her dessert spoon and said, "I'm sorry I think we've wasted all this time. I'm really not a great date, Peter."

"Oh, I wouldn't say that." He said slowly. He laid his glass down and leaned forward slightly. With a smile, he added, "You are beautiful to behold. If only to look at you for an hour or two I would do this again and again."

Flustered, a blush crept from her neck to her ears.

"Oh, I think YOU are a very sly man for saying that."

"Am I sly?"

"Yes, you are."

"I apologize, I meant every word."

She couldn't look at him for a long moment and fidgeted with her napkin. She longed to look at her watch but didn't want to offend him. Rebecca was beginning to crumble, and she knew that he knew it.

"I'm going to have to make it an early night, my dear Rebecca," Peter said finally. "I have a lot of work to do tomorrow morning. I'll pay the bill, and then I'll take you home, okay?"

"Okay."

Rebecca felt a wave of dismay. He praised her beauty but said he wanted to take her home early. It disappointed her deeply, and she wasn't sure why. Her face looked sad as he wrote his signature on the check.

He got up and held out his hand for hers. Rebecca put her hand in his, and they walked out of the restaurant without another word.

"Are you okay still?" Peter asked out of the blue as they drove quickly through the streets of the West End.

"Yes. Just a bit chilly here."

He glanced down at her and noted that she was wearing a very fetching dress - almost like a sheath that hugged her body making it look even sleeker. She seemed to be like a fairy tale heroine to him, and Peter tried not to let his thoughts wander any further.

He kept his hands on the wheel and returned his attention to the road. It was almost nine o'clock in the evening. Soon they navigated the neighborhood of Rebecca's flat. At the corner, the Tube subway station stood empty of people.

"We're almost home," Peter said in an attempt at conversation.

"Good - I think it's a nice thing to take me out for dinner, Peter - " Rebecca was about to say something more, but the bright flames lit up by the side of the road as they passed.

"What the devil - ?" Peter's car swerved. The bomb - which it was - had detonated just after they passed the Tube station.

"Oh my God, was that what I thought it was?" She asked, looking back at it.

Peter stepped on the gas and sped off, knowing that the bomb blast would likely shake the foundations of the buildings nearby. "Yes, it was a bomb, I'm afraid."

Peter looked in his rearview mirror and saw

flames licking out from the corner where they just passed moments ago. People ran from all directions, out of the pubs, out of coffee shops, out of grocery stores and into the streets. The dark gloom of the night was dispelled by the rising fire that soon became too hot for anyone nearby to stand.

The blare of sirens soon filled the night air. Almost all streets had become impassable. Finally, after waiting for two minutes at a standstill, Peter decided to park his car on the curb. "We can't go further - there's much to much gridlock. I'm sorry Rebecca, we have to walk you home."

"I'm fine with that. Thank you."

They got out and walked quickly away from the car. He held her hand in a tight grip, and his eyes glanced everywhere, looking for suspicious characters.

She gripped her purse tightly under her arm and felt glad that she wasn't wearing high heels. Her tall height was only half a foot less than Peter's at this point. Rebecca finally became aware of how close they were to being casualties. That was when she began to feel afraid and her eyes teared up. She wished for some comfort, and as though he read her mind, Peter put his arm around her shoulder and herded her to her building.

Peter's cell rang in his pocket, but he ignored it. It wasn't for him to attend to this as his status was to investigate after the police had had their look at the damages. They came to her floor, and soon they were in her flat. Peter took off his jacket and decided they needed something to drink. "I think we need a strong drink, don't you?"

"I'm not sure what we have in the pantry." She

replied, slipping out of her shoes and walking to the window to see whether she could see anything.

He saw her and said in a sharp voice, "Don't do that. Let's stay out of the window for now. You never can tell who's around and if there's anyone involved with this bombing attack."

"Oh!" Rebecca stepped away from the window and joined him in the kitchen.

"I found a bottle of brandy. Do you have any glassware?"

"Here." She had opened a cupboard and brought out the glasses.

He poured them both a stiff drink and they sipped the fiery liquid in silence.

Peter's cell rang again, but he silenced it. He said nothing about the call, but he knew it came from Moorehead.

He turned to see her sit on the edge of a stool and regard him with eyes that were frightened. "You know that bomb is only a few hundred feet from my flat."

"Yes."

"I've not been listening to the latest, but this has to be at least the third in a row?"

"I'd say you are accurate."

"Maybe I'm crazy about wanting to live in London. How do you cope with this type of thing happening? In your own backyard?"

"You cope as well as can be."

"It's not comforting me at all."

"Likely they will call off work for the day tomorrow. Unless you work across town and then they'll have it as usual. In your case, you'd have to go to work. You can take the bus instead or a taxi." He almost added that he could take her to work. And he did, "I could take you to work, Rebecca. I don't want you walking around for a few days in this area particularly."

Her eyes widened, and her smile was grateful. "Oh, Peter, that would be great!"

Peter tried not to look at her too much. Her beauty was beginning to tear down his defenses.

"Well, I think - " He almost said he was going to leave, but it didn't make sense to him. Instead, he put his glass down and walked to her side. He pulled her to him and kissed her lightly on the lips. "I think I like that." He murmured.

"So do I." She smiled trustingly up at him.

"Then I have to do it again," he smiled back and kissed her mouth again, this time with a great deal of hunger behind it. Her response was equally hungry. They kept on kissing until he became aware of a growing need for her. He felt against him, pliant and soft, and yet solid under his palms. He murmured her name as their kisses became urgent. "I want to make love to you," he said in a whisper.

She threw all her worries to the wind. The thought of Elena was a distant thing in her mind. He pulled her to him, his questing hands slid down her back, his fingers seeking underneath her dress until he found her bare flesh. She arched her back as he fondled her. "No – ," she could barely breathe.

"I want you."

He pulled her dress over her head and she stood almost naked in her bra before him. He took in a sharp breath when he beheld her. Peter's mind went out of control and he pulled her into the bedroom and closed the door.

They made love in her bed. She was beautiful and eager to make him know that she wanted him as much as he wanted her. Her body smelled delicious to Peter and he desired her more than any woman he had ever had. Their lovemaking became so intense that their breathing became ragged, almost panting in desire. Peter fucked her almost continuously and she clung to him, making small whimpering sounds in his ear. When they were fully satisfied, they held each other close and Peter felt her body relax in his grasp. Soon, Rebecca fell into a deep slumber.

He held her to him all night long, and when she stirred, he made love to her once again, this time delighting in her body with his lips and tongue so that she became aflame with desire for him.

"You are making me so close to bursting," she whispered.

"You are making me die," he replied.

"You've no idea how I want you," she confessed

shyly.

"Then we're even."

Peter and Rebecca slept deeply, their limbs still entwined, through the night. The sirens had long gone and the night was strangely quiet. Peter slept soundly as did Rebecca. But the stirrings of a thought came to him in the wee hours of the morning, making him open his eyes and survey the tousled and naked figure of Rebecca next to him.

Peter lay on his back and stared into the darkness. His mind was tormenting him. What he felt for Rebecca was nothing like he had felt for any other woman before. He pulled Rebecca into his embrace and she stirred and then snuggled against him, trustingly like a child. *Oh my*, Peter sighed to himself.

Chapter Twelve

Peter was on the phone when Rebecca finally awoke the next morning. She heard the alarm go off and found that Peter had left the bed. She got up, dressed quickly in a silk robe, and slid into her slippers before heading to the kitchen.

"I need a few hours to get there," Peter was saying as she passed him on the way to make coffee. "Yes. I will check that out. I'll talk to you soon. Bye."

Peter bent his head as if to ring off but the voice on the other end still droned on. Peter looked quickly at Rebecca and smiled at her absently. His eyes rolled upwards as if to say that the person he was talking to was being a bore. Rebecca smothered a giggle and worked on making a pot of coffee.

She mouthed to him, "Coffee?" Peter shook his head and mouthed back "Tea." Rebecca smiled brightly and dispatched the coffee pot and instead reached for the tea kettle.

"Look, Watkins, I've already said I'm sorry. I will take care of it soon as I get back on the road." Peter turned as if to hide his conversation from her ears. "Listen, why don't we both meet at ten a.m." He glanced at his wristwatch. "Yes, that is in three and a half hours. Is that ok? No? Ok, fine. I'll get there as soon as I've had my tea. Is that good? Ok, fine.

Thanks." He rang off and pocketed his cell.

"Sounds like you are going to be in for a difficult morning?" She spoke with hesitancy.

"No, that's just him. He's a bastard, sometimes." He laughed and then went to her side, gathering her in his arms. "I loved last night. Believe that, will you?"

Rebecca let him nuzzle her neck. "I wonder what Elena might say."

"Oh. Well, that's a bit of an awkward topic."

"I bet." Rebecca nevertheless let him hold her as she fixed the tea bags into the Brown Betty. "I don't know what it is but you are a puzzle and I had to let you have me despite the knowledge."

"So you don't care that she's engaged to me." He turned her around to look at her.

"I might not care but if she knew then I'll be in a heap of trouble, Mr. Reed." Rebecca's eyes were serious. "I've never poached someone else's man. I won't want to do it now."

"So you regret last night?"

Rebecca sighed. "Look let's have tea first."

"Why don't we discuss this later?"

"I'm not sure whether that is going to happen. I feel somewhat of a horrible guilt feeling. Is that what you feel too?"

Peter looked serious as well. "No. I don't feel any guilt."

"Wow. I don't know Peter. What are you all about?"

"I'm not sure what I'm all about these days. I think you have given me a spell, a spell that I could ward off, but I've let it happen. Now I'm sunk into you and I feel rather unstable."

"I am sorry if I've done that. I am not a witch,

Peter. I am woefully an unwilling prey to the people in my life."

"Like whom?"

"Oh, my ex." Rebecca slid out of his arms.

"Your ex. Tell me about him." Peter raked his hair with his fingers, feeling as though he was going to get into more trouble talking about her life. It wasn't a great feeling, being somewhat roped into this woman's life. It made him even more aware that his calling as a spy was on thin ice.

"If you have time -"

"I have time. Well, let's say I have as much time as you can give me. I want to know." Again, something in his gut made him feel worse than ever. "Look Rebecca, I am a poor cad and have always been. I've had a lot of affairs and then I've had a job for a number of years where my feelings didn't matter a damn. Now, you're here and I"ve made you very much a part of me somehow. I know, we've only made love once. But I am trying to keep my head and it's not helping with you looking so beautiful."

She flushed, almost embarrassed that someone as handsome and yet rough around the edges could say this to her. After Cor, Peter was a revelation. "I'm listening. You are a cad, you said. I am a spoiled girl from Connecticut, with parents who have always kept an eye on me. I ran off with a man who I thought I loved. But he was worse than a cad. He was a gambler and took drugs. I hope you aren't either?"

"No, not really. I do gamble but I'm not a drug addict." Again his stomach felt like lurching. Why am I prevaricating? His thought came to him.

"I see. Well, that is me. I'm an innocent. I am. I have not much sense, a lot of times. But I thought living in London was going to be a new start for me. I'd be on my own, have my own flat, pay my own bills, have a job, do all that independent women my age want to do well. And, fall in love. An impossible thing, from what my parents think. They think I'm supposed to go back home."

Peter's eyes looked sharply at her. "You might want to do that. You should know London is a bad place for innocent girls like you. I am not joking here."

His stare made her start. "Oh. I can tell you are serious. So - what about us, then? Is this it? I suppose it's best if we end it here."

"I think it might be best." He spoke slowly. HIs insides were getting him in worse trouble. It almost was unbearable to him to say goodbye to their budding relationship. He had a good time baiting her, seducing her, and making love to her. Now she was saying what he should have said. It made him unhappy to have an innocent American girl tell him flatly that she might have to end this affair.

"Alright." Rebecca heard the kettle rattle and whistle. "Do you then think we ought to end it now? A one night stand." The words made her lips tremble. "God, I hate that. I can't believe I had a one night stand. I am so very sorry." She started to cry and he stood looking at her helplessly.

He felt as though hands were grabbing him to keep him from going to her side. He pushed that aside and went to her. "Look, my dear Rebecca, we have to say so long. You need to go back to America. Find a decent chap, and marry him and have a lot of babies. It isn't for us - perhaps I have to look at how my life is - it - I need to - I - Hell, I can't stand this either."

She turned away and he took her to him again.

They stood mute and yet they didn't attempt to step away from each other.

Finally Peter made the supreme effort to step away. "I'll have to pass on the tea for now. Maybe we - er - I have to leave this here. I can't want to end it yet. I am a cad, let me be a cad for you. I'll have to go now. Maybe we can see each other sometime - perhaps."

Rebecca wiped her tears and still kept her face averted. "If you wish."

"I don't want you to think I'm going hurt your feelings." He bent to lift her chin and gazed into her eyes. "You do have feelings for me?"

She didn't answer. They paused and then he turned to leave.

"I'll call you."

He left her then and she went to the kettle where she fiddled with the tea bag.

The telephone rang and the answering machine came on. The voice of Elena came through.

"Rebecca? It's me, Elena. Why don't you pick up the phone? I heard about the bombing. Are you ok? I want you to call me. I sent you a text. Goodbye."

The smoke was still in the air as Peter stepped out of Rebecca's building. His eyes scanned the street as he walked quickly towards his car. The view of the subway entrance was obscured by the presence of London police cars and several police personnel were crowded about the blackened entrance. No other pedestrians were present. Peter surmised that this entrance was closed off, as per police protocol. He did not go there. He slipped into his drivers seat and shut the door. He sat there for a moment, going over the scenes of last night with Rebecca. He closed his eyes and savored the lovemaking, bringing back his emotions to surface in his heart. He felt a push to tell Watkins. But he felt more the urge to go home to his flat and make some decisions before he would confront Watkins.

He could envision the scene where he would turn in his gun but the warring thought made it hard - that thought was the sworn duty of his type to fight the enemy wherever that may be.

Yet, the enemy had stolen a march on his plans last night. He was making love to a very attractive woman when he should have reported the crime and made arrangements to survey the location of this dastardly terrorist malfeasance.

He opened his eyes and started his car. Slowly

he pulled out of his space and sped into the highway taking him away. Where he wanted to go was nowhere. He became aware that there was no other place to be but where Rebecca was. It cost him a great deal, this thought. It cost him a great deal already. His operation. His plan. Gone in a matter of seconds one his lips tasted Rebecca's.

The phone rang and obliterated all thought about Rebecca. It was Watkins.

"Where are you now?" Watkins voice was acerbic.

"I'm driving."

"Where are you going?"

"I need to check on something. I will come by when I'm ready."

"I want you to come soon. The others are eager to commiserate."

He stifled a groan. "I am not ready to face them."

"What's eating at you?"

"Nothing. I need to talk to you. Can we meet somewhere?"

"Now?" Watkins sounded incredulous.

"Yes. I thought the battery park by the Bridge."

"Ok. I'll see you there in a few minutes. I'm actually taking a drive to the office."

"Good."

Chapter Thirteen

Watkins was pacing the ground when Peter approached
him. He was deep in thought, Watkins was. He glanced
at his wristwatch and then stuck his hands into his Mac.
The winds were fierce this morning and everyone
seemed to have deserted the place. The water that
lapped against the border wall were dark grey. The
Tower Bridge gleamed oddly in the dark sun. Nobody
heard Peter approach.

"Watkins."

Watkins looked around and saw Peter walking towards him. "Oh, good." He looked at his face and saw nothing to let him know what was in Peter's mind. "You're very tardy. You've had all night to tell us. I know you were in the vicinity." Watkins growled at him and gave him a fierce look.

"That's not possible."

"Oh? Do you think you're immune to watchers?" Watkins demanded. "Think again. Who was that woman you escorted home?"

"Damn!" Peter exploded. "Now, look here, this is my personal life. It's OFF LIMITS."

"Not when there's a recent bombing at Charing Cross and YOU were there and said ZERO about it. Damn, Peter, I could just sack you right now for omission of duty."

"Ok, ok. Let's start over again. I can explain."

"Start now. I have a few things to do." Watkins looked meaningfully at his watch and then looked at Peter expectantly.

"Look, I asked this girl out. She's Elena's roommate. She and I hit it off."

"So you bedded her last night."

"Must you be so crass? I did have a moment of passion but that's over now. I had to - " Peter bit his lip. "Look, I'm on this case and I will see it through."

"NO," said Watkins. "This girl is a distraction and she could easily be a casualty. How can you tell me - assure me - that this girl isn't going to be a part of the collateral damage from your operation? Can you squarely say this to me? Who's she anyway?"

"I told you. She's an American who is trying out living in this country."

"Fat lot it will do if she's going to be dead because YOU forgot to warn us this terrorist group was going to hit."

"This terror bombing was NOT in the plans that we know of." Peter said flatly.

"Then that is even MORE abominable. YOU had NO IDEA?"

"I did not know it would happen last night. And I had nobody let me know that this was in anyone's plan.

"I want Revenor tailed all day and all night and I want to know what else he's planning. Ditch the girl, Reed. I warn you."

Reed said nothing.

"Are you deaf? Tell me you'll tell her it's over."

Reed stared back at him. Somewhere in the depths of his grey-blue eyes there was a flicker of something that was akin to anger and despair.

"I'm not sure that it is over. I will tell her we need to cool it."

"No, my dear chap, it's not done this way. Hate to tell you dear boy, but this woman could be turned. I fear the worst. You need to turn this operation over to someone else."

"Who would it be?"

"What about that CIA man? He's ok with this I'm sure, what do you think of him?"

Peter snorted. "No."

"Then I'll have to ask someone else your peer to do this. Go and do what you want to do. I'll let them know you've taken a leave of absence. If this makes you happy then I will do what I can. But you can't put your indecision and your woman in harms way."

Peter paced the ground and then stared out to the water's edge.

Watkins expectantly waited. When Peter said nothing, he walked off.

Chapter Fourteen

That same morning, while news of the bombing splashed around the world's newscasts and press, Rebecca made her way up to her office in the hospital, avoiding any or all who might be wishing to discuss the horrible happening with her or anyone around. Her head bowed down as she exited the elevators, leaving behind the chatter of those who were still steaming in tempers about the lack of security anymore in the great city of London.

When she entered the office, she found it empty. Mystified, Rebecca went to her desk and started her workday. She noticed that the coffee maker was empty and still clean, the decanter was still in the sink waiting to be rinsed out. Rising again from her chair, she went to the sink and started to make the morning coffee.

Her mind started to think back to her fantastic experience being made love to by Peter Reed the night before. It was so much a forceful memory that imprinted itself on her being and all of her thoughts could only be impressed at her release of passion that Peter ignited. Her face became scarlet at the memory and she tried not to dwell on it for fear that somebody would come in and find her looking flushed.

Yet, the next memory that came to her was that coolness that Peter exhibited towards her the morning after. Her mind told her that this man was not trustworthy. She didn't say, she told herself gratefully, those words "I love you" - no, those words weren't ready to be spoken not even in her own mind.

Peter made an excuse that his work beckoned and merely took her to a different subway stop so he could go back to his office that morning.

She finished the coffee preparations and left it to brew. She washed her cup and dried it, still looking sober. *I'm so lost and confused*, she told herself miserably.

The telephone rang at her desk so she hurried to pick it up. "Social Work, Rebecca speaking." She spoke in her lowered tones.

"Hello, Rebecca, it's Cor. How are you doing, my love?"

She grimaced and almost hung up. "Fine, Cor. I'm really busy now."

"It won't take long, my dear, I wanted to see how you are. I heard about the bombing right around where your flat is. I wanted to rush over but I saw on the telly that the place was crazy with police cars and ambulances. Even this morning!" He went on to add, "I hope that you weren't alone or anything when it happened. I can't imagine how terrifying it might have been for you. Dear Rebecca, you really ought to live with me. I will keep you safe, I really will."

She bit back a retort that refuted his last statement. Instead, Rebecca replied, "I am fine, Cor. I am sure things will sort itself out with this terrorist act. I wasn't alone, no. I am fine. Now, why don't you just go and leave me alone. I am serious, Cor. Leave me alone!"

"But Rebecca - "

"No, just goodbye!"

"Wait - Wait!" He said but she slammed the phone down and sat down in a rush. Her heart beat fast, mostly from her reverie about Peter but now because of the rising temper she felt at the very sound of Cor's voice. How she felt anything for him was a wonder, she thought miserably.

The door opened and Mrs. Bellingham bustled in, muttering to herself. "I ask you, how could this sort of thing happen any more these days? Isn't it time the authorities made some headway and kept us all safe? I ask you!" She looked up and saw Rebecca looking at her soberly. "Hello, Rebecca, how are you? I hope you had a good evening." Then she froze and then said with a great gasp, "Oh, no! YOU live just around the corner from that subway stop! I am so very sad that it happened near your place. You should have called in and told someone you wanted to rest or find some sort of refuge somewhere. We would have understood!"

Mrs. Bellingham went to Rebecca's side and gave her a pat on the shoulder. Being so much older than Rebecca, she resisted the urge to hug the young woman. She stood at her side, with words attempting to spill out and give sympathy but they didn't come out.

Rebecca looked up at her and smiled finally with a winning smile. "No, I am fine. I actually wasn't exactly that frightened."

"Oh! Well, were you at your flat? Or were you out and didn't see it happen?"

"I was not at my flat, no. Actually, I was with a friend. So I wasn't alone when it happened."

Mrs. Bellingham's wrinkled brow relaxed. "Oh, good! I am so very glad you weren't alone. It was a good friend, I hope."

"Yes, he was. A good friend, yes." Rebecca nodded, almost convinced that Peter Reed was a good friend indeed.

"Good. Good good good." Mrs. Bellingham went over to her desk and started to put her purse and umbrella away. She prattled on about other things and didn't really say much more about Rebecca until she had poured herself a cup of coffee. "Rebecca," she said in a voice that belied her interest. "What friend was this? Was this your room mate?"

"No. It was someone else." Rebecca replied, skimming the emails on her computer.

"Oh."

"Yes, it was a new friend - someone I met the other day."

"Oh, so was this a man or woman?"

"It was a man. He works for the City. I - " she stopped and looked closely at an email. Her eyes took on a darker hue. "We had dinner and then he took me home."

"Oh." Mrs Bellingham said again. She took her coffee back to her desk and gingerly placed it on the caster next to her mouse.

The silence made it clear that Rebecca was not about to divulge any more information about Peter. Rebecca hated gossipy women and this conversation was beginning to take a little turn into something lurid.

The thought was disgusting enough to Rebecca that she got up and said, "I am summoned to see Mr. Khalid again. He is really now about to be discharged."

"Take the check out documents dear and make sure he signs it. We don't want the patients running off without telling us they are satisfied with their treatment here." Mrs. Bellingham said gruffly.

"Sure." Rebecca said as she picked up the file
and went out the door.

Mrs Bellingham sat back and stirred her coffee.
A little smile came over her lips and this is how Mr Ivey
found her.

"Bellingham? What are you smiling at?" He had
entered without a sound and fairly shook Mrs
Bellingham out of her own reverie.

"I don't really know, Mr. Ivey." Said Mrs
Bellingham. "But our dear Rebecca has found herself a
gentleman."

Mr Ivey shook off the raindrops off his raincoat
before he hung it on the door. "Oh? That's nice, then.
She's better off without that Corcoran fellow."

"How do you know about that man?" Mrs
Bellingham demanded, wiping the coffee from her

blouse.

"Oh, I know everything, Mrs Bellingham." Mr. Ivey smiled, putting a finger by his nose. "Now, why don't we go and do some work and let's try to keep ourselves out of trouble. Lord knows we have enough trouble outside."

He went into his office and closed the door with a snap.

Chapter Fifteen

Heathrow airport was massively crowded when Sophia
and Leo's flight arrived. They waited for the rush of
passengers out of the plane until they could calmly get
their carryons and then proceeded to leave for the airport
interior. Sophia's eyes were big with excitement and
surveyed the crowd as they walked purposefully to the
customs department. Leo looked non-plussed as he felt
in his pocket for his passport. They arrived at the

customs and got through without a fuss due to Leo's frequent flights to and from London since he became Chief of Surgery at the hospital back in the USA.

"I'm so excited, Leo dear. It's like I'm on a holiday." Sophia said with a hushed excited voice.

"You are on a holiday, my dear." Leo said with a smile.

"Oh," she chuffed him on the sleeve. "You know what I mean!"

They both laughed and then became serious as they followed the rest of the arrivals to get their luggage and then find transportation to their hotels.

They were finally in the taxicab and Leo tried to open his eyes wider in order to keep alert. "Boy, the trip wasn't too bad but I hate taking early flights."

"Leo, you are a trouper." Sophia said, her face

staring out the window as the taxi rounded through the A6. "Do you really have only tomorrow for your lecture? I would love us to take a little tour around. It's been a long time since I have been in London. Look, there's the London Eye."

"Thanks my love. Yes that is it." His gaze followed hers. "I do only have tomorrow as day with the Royal College of Surgeons. I will have to make it clear to our daughter that she ought to at least meet you for lunch and then if she can, find a way to leave early -"

"Oh, she said she will come and stay with me for the day. Her boss said she could."

"Good."

They sat in companionable silence. Sophia's attention was fixed on the different attractions that made London an exceptional city for tourists. Leo, having been there enough times, closed his eyes and tried to think. "You know," he finally said. "You and Rebecca need to discuss her decision to dump Corcoran and then live on here in this very chaotic city. Tomorrow."

Sophia sat back and her face sobered. "We can discuss this tonight, surely, Leo?"

"I only want us to be focused on our intention to come and visit. We are NOT here for the conference tomorrow. I want to make our daughter aware that she is living in a very bad place at a very bad time."

She glanced at the back of the cab driver before answering. "Ok, I will talk to her tomorrow. Now, why don't we enjoy the cab ride?"

Leo sighed and then closed his eyes once again. He didn't want to speak much more and he put his lips together tightly in a firm line.

The hotel loomed up and finally they were getting checked in. Leo and Sophia took the elevators with the bellboy trailing them with their luggage. It was a brightly decorated hotel, and flowers adorned the lobby and hallway. Tourists came in and out. A gaggle of teenagers wearing a uniform jersey rushed past them and almost bumped Leo. The atmosphere was that of a great party where happy and excited tourists converged, then parted ways and climbed into buses and other transportation to tour the city.

Their room was well appointed and spoke of Leo and Sophia's wealth. The hotel was a five star hotel. They had a suite and everything was spacious and had soft carpeting.

Sophia immediately checked the bathroom and saw that it was a bit cramped. She sighed and then went back to the living area. "It's not bad but I could use more elbow room in that bathroom."

Leo glanced up at her and smiled quickly. "That's European hotel for you. I am sure we will survive."

"Yes." She frowned and patted her hair unconsciously. "I will take a shower tonight so that you can have the bathroom for yourself tomorrow. How's that?"

Leo laughed finally. "My dear girl, you are a soul of kindness."

She giggled despite her age. "Dear Leo, you know I take hours to get ready. Ha ha."

They hugged and then Leo heard the phone ring. He went to pick it up. "Hello." He spoke into the receiver.

"Daddy?"

"Rebecca darling, how are you? Where are

you?"

"I'm at work still. I've got another hour to work here. How was your trip?" Her voice sounded high pitched.

Leo frowned at this. "Are you alright, Rebecca? You don't sound like yourself."

"Oh," she replied and then she added, "I'm fine. It's been a bit hectic here. There was a bombing yesterday. I am surprised you hadn't heard.

"Bombing?" Leo echoed. Sophia looked around and her face fell with anxiety.

"Yes. It's been so chaotic here. It was actually near my flat."

"Near your flat?" His voice became dark with concern. "Damn it, Rebecca, why didn't you tell us?'

"Well, because I - because I was - ah - because I had - " her voice trailed.

"Well, never mind that. Look, why don't we have dinner tonight? I'll take a cab to your place and then we all can find a place to eat."

Sophia nodded approval at his suggestion.

Rebecca's voice became more relaxed. "That would be fine. I will be at home sometime before six p.m."

"Good. Let's see each other round then. I need your cell phone number unless," he raised an eyebrow at Sophia. "Your mother has it?"

Sophia nodded again. "Yes, I've got it." She shook her head mentally at how her husband seemed to be at a loss for simple things like cell phone numbers but did excellent work as a heart surgeon. Sophia grinned at Leo as he talked to their daughter.

"She has it. She'll call you and then we can get together, ok? You're ok aren't you?"

"Yes, Daddy. I'm fine."

He hung up and let out a sigh. "I'm steamed. That is really enough. I want her home soon."

"Ok, just calm down. We will discuss it. She has to see she cannot stay here."

Leo paced the carpeted floor and finally he threw his hands up. "I'm going to take a nap and try to relax. Too much of this. God, I'm getting old."

Sophia watched him as he took off his coat and tossed it over a chair. They moved silently in the room getting out of their outerwear and tossing aside their shoes. Sophia tried to unpack but her agitation got the better of her and she too decided to lie down on the bed and let the tensions of the day flow out from her.

Chapter Sixteen

Rebecca was at home early that day mainly due to having received a phone call. It came from Peter. He caught her right after she had hung up from her call with her father.

"I hope you're doing better today." Peter's voice sounded suave to her ears.

"Yes. I'm ok. How are you?"

"Not so well." He masked his emotions so well

it came out without much of a nuance that he was in the throes of figuring out what he needed to do with his work and with her.

"I'm going to see my parents tonight." Rebecca informed him. "They just came for a week's stay. Daddy's giving a paper at the Royal Surgeons' conference."

"Oh I see. He's a doctor, is he? A surgeon?"

"Yes."

"Look Rebecca, we need to talk."

Her heart was gripped by that statement. She felt sick. "About what?" She aimed to sound nonchalant.

"Us."

"Oh, us."

"Can we see each other later? How long will you be with your parents tonight?"

"I can't really say. Perhaps a couple of hours.

We'll be meeting for dinner."

He paused. Then he said, "Look, I'll give you a call later, and then I'll come and see you. How does that sound?"

"I think that's fine." She tried to head him off at the pass. "Look, Peter, if it's about the last time we saw each other, I don't want you to get any ideas. I'm sure we can be friends. I know that you and Elena are engaged. It was - "

"No, no, I don't want this hashed out over a telephone call."

She felt a sting of anger go through her. "I don't intend to stand here and get ditched. I won't see you tonight. Good bye."

She hung up and proceeded to burst into tears.

Peter stared at his phone before he also hung up. It made

his face look so stern that his coworker, Moorhead took a double take when he glanced up. "Anything wrong?"

"Just about everything." Peter ground out evenly.

"Ah. I won't pry then."

"Don't."

Moorhead sat back in his chair and looked at Peter consideringly. "I think women are the bastard of life."

Peter ignored this and proceeded to put on his jacket.

"I'm sorry. She must be a really good girl."

"What do you know about her?"

"I've heard some talk."

Peter's eyes were sharp on Moorhead. "Oh? What sort of talk?"

"God, I'm sorry Peter, I overheard Watkins

talking. I didn't mean to."

"Who was he talking to?"

"Whitehall."

"Oh hell."

"Is that really it for you? Are you quitting?"

He looked at Moorhead and shrugged. "I don't know. I think I might."

"So Watkins wanted to get someone else to replace you, is what I gathered."

"Did Watkins know you were there listening?"

Moorhead laughed. "I don't think he was. He was having a bath and talking on his phone. I have a bug in his bathroom. Just standard operating procedure."

"You bugger." Peter said with a hint of a smile. "Look, I'm not sure what I'll do. I am screwing up royally with this operation and I am now hoping I can dislodge my so-called engagement to Elena without her passing it on to that scumbag Revenor."

"I won't tell."

"You better not or I'll hunt you down and stuff your face and throw you into gaol."

Moorhead looked at him with a terrified stare. "I won't I promise." He became agitated. "Look I'm a shit and I plant bugs for a living. I won't do you any harm. I like that American girl. She's a great girl from all I can tell."

Peter was silent for a moment.

"Look here, I think if you want to get out of this maze we call MI5 it would be fine. You'll have to go through a ton of debriefing and then clearance and then maybe they'll try to keep you anyway. I don't know how you can ever escape this place even if you retire out of here. They'll get you back in on an innocuous question, a ploy, then you're all theirs all over again.

That girl is going to be in the way. That's what I think."

Peter walked to the door and then paused. He stood for a moment and then he left, shutting the door quietly after him.

Chapter Seventeen

Hopsey's was where the Bartholomew family came together for dinner. It was not a great place in terms of food but the ambience was more private and they found a table closer to the back where Leo could expound on the finer points of leaving England for The USA.

They dispensed with ordering as soon as possible and then Leo leaned back in his seat to observe his only child. He saw her looking quieter than he remembered.

Her face was thin and drawn. She looked as though she lost weight everywhere. It wasn't totally a bad picture and he envisioned her to be vastly attractive to men who liked blondes and American ones in particular. He sighed and let his wife do most of the talking. For her part, Sophia commented also on how Rebecca had lost weight.

"Surely you can't have lost this much weight since we last saw you?" Asked Sophia with a reproachful stare.

"Mom, I'm ok. Really, I'm ok." Rebecca said, plaiting her napkin on the table.

"Well, are you earning enough money? Is it that expensive here for you? How much does it cost of keep your flat anyway?" Leo interjected, unable to help himself.

"Oh, I earn enough money. It's not as though it's

like how much I earned back at Yale New Haven."

Sophia glanced at her husband. "No, it wouldn't be. Leo saw to that, didn't you."

Leo tried not to look at his wife. "Let's not talk about that, shall we?" He leaned forward. "So, what about this flat? I'd like to take a look at it later. Ok? Is it safe there? That bombing, lord, have mercy, I am not at all happy that it took place within walking distance of your flat!"

Rebecca drew herself up in an attempt to defend herself. "I'm fine, Daddy. I am. I had someone with me and it was ok."

Sophia looked at her with a gleam in her eye. "Oh, someone?"

"Who is that?" Leo asked sharply.

"He's a friend. His name is Peter. Peter Reed."

Leo read that look on his daughter face and

started to get nervous. "Ok, so he's a friend. What does he do?"

"He works for a law firm, from what I gather."

"Where did he meet you?" Sophia asked.

Fortunately, their first course arrived. They all sat back and let the waiter serve the salad. Leo looked annoyed at the interruption.

"So, where did you meet?"

"He's a friend of a friend," Rebecca replied slowly.

The parents let that sink in and they ate in silence. Sensing a relief Rebecca kept her own silence.

"Did he say anything about this bombing? Did he - " Sophia started to say.

"He was there and kept me company until it was all clear."

Leo knew his daughter enough to guess that this

was a statement constructed to keep her privacy. So, he thought, there's a man in her life. It wasn't Corcoran, that one whom she dumped. "Ok, good. How good a friend is he? Does he come by and see you? Or is he merely someone who dated you once?"

Rebecca gasped. She realized her father read her correctly. "Yes, he has only dated me once."

Sophia kept her silence and listened but then she finally spoke. "I'm still hoping you'll consider coming home, dear. I don't like that you were close to this terrorist attack. I don't think you were really planning to stay here, were you?"

"I'm hoping to stay as long as I can."

Leo set his salad plate aside. "I'm losing my appetite."

"Oh, Leo, there's more to come. You need to eat. You'll be busy tomorrow." Sophia said quietly.

"I'm going to give you three weeks to make up your mind, Miss Rebecca." Leo said with a stern look in his eyes. "You will come back at the end of this time. I won't take "No" for an answer. Is that clear?"

Rebecca stared back at her father. "No, I don't like that. I am grown up and can find life a good thing here. I have friends - friends - " she faltered. "I think it will be a great life here."

Both her parents looked at each other. Sophia spoke. "Why not enjoy the dinner, dear Leo. Let's make it a happy reunion. Rebecca appears to enjoy life in London. I think this Peter person is a possibly good influence on our daughter." She turned to Rebecca. "Why don't you invite Peter to lunch with us tomorrow - he won't mind seeing your mother, will he? Is he nice? How about that for starters? I don't expect him to marry you, but I WOULD like to thank him for being with you when this attack happened."

Leo studied his daughter's face as she digested this suggestion. Then a smile tugged at his mouth.

"Well I can ask him, but he's really a busy man."

"Just ask him. I'll be busy with delivering my paper. Let's try that and see." Leo said, almost relaxing in his chair. "I'll have to keep in touch via cell and then we can regroup later, Sophia."

Sophia nodded. The second course came and then they were busy with that. Rebecca, feeling a strange relief wash over her, dug into her main course with relish. She ate as though she hadn't eaten in days. Sophia noticed her eat with gusto and worried again.

"I'll see you tomorrow then, right, Rebecca?"

"Of course. I'll take a cab to your hotel and then we can both do some sight seeing. How's that?"

"Maybe you shouldn't tire out your mother too

much tomorrow. Let's say you can have a leisurely lunch, and then have more time to catch up." Leo smiled and looked at both. "How does that sound?"

The others said nothing, one because she didn't want to catch up and the other one was trying to keep a fair distance from her now grown daughter who seems to have found another man that could keep her in London.

Chapter Eighteen

Rebecca said goodbye to her parents after they had

repaired to her flat and inspected it with great care,

commenting on this and that and summing up the place

was good and sturdy. Sophia looked brightly at her and

stated that she wanted them to go shopping sometime

and pick out some nice linens and curtains. Rebecca was

elated as she felt as though her world was back and her

parents' company gave her such a balm to her sad heart,

after Peter had spoken to her the day before.

Leo was less excited, being a man and merely made sure that the telephone was working and the bathroom and toilet were also in order.

Once satisfied, the two parents left her and hailed a cab which took them back to their hotel.

Leo glanced at his wife once they were in the cab and spoke wearily. "I'm afraid she is happy enough here."

"Leo, I think she is outwardly fine but I sense some sort of trouble. This Peter fellow is not too good if he is already - ah - well, I feel as though something's not right there yet."

"Is it really so soon after they've gone out the first time?"

Sophia looked out the window and sighed. "I'll talk to her some more about this guy. I'm really a bit tired out from the trip. I'll be glad to have the lights out tonight."

Leo found a piece of gum in his pocket and proceeded to chew it. He relished the taste of the burst of flavor in his mouth and felt as though he was back somehow in his mind in his own country. He said aloud, "I'm wondering if this place has gum for sale. I feel as though I'm needing to have this here more often."

"Gum?"

"Yes, gum." He looked at her blankly.

"I am sure they sell it. I've never known you to chew gum, Leo." She smiled to herself. "Is this how you conduct yourself when you travel nowadays?"

He laughed softly. "No, well, I guess I do - it's a bit like home, you know. Baseball and stuff like that."

They sat in companionable silence until they arrived at the hotel.

At the same time, Rebecca was getting ready to go to bed and had her pajamas on. She went to the living room to choose a magazine to read and found it. As she walked back to her bedroom, she heard a knock.

She decided not to answer it and went past through the doorway.

The knock came once again and a familiar voice called. "Rebecca, it's me, Peter."

She went to the door and opened it. He looked at her and walked past her to the middle of the living room.

"Sorry, I didn't call first. You're ready to turn in?"

Rebecca looked at him as he faced her and smiled slightly. "I am. I didn't want to talk to you at all.

If you wish to say what's on your mind, go ahead."

"I'm really sorry that I have to talk to you about this. I have to explain a few things about me."

"Go on."

He went to the couch and sat down. "Can we sit a while and talk?"

Rebecca went to sit at the other end of the couch and looked toward the kitchen. "Ok. What do you want to talk to me about?"

Peter paused. Then he asked her, "Does Elena tell you about me much?"

"She has not."

"Not even what I do with her these days?"

Rebecca reddened and shook her head. "No, she doesn't do much talking about her private life. She hardly is here and if she is she has a different schedule than mine."

There was a long pause as though he were turning something over in his mind. Finally he said, "I'm not able to keep our relationship at the level you wish to have."

"And what level is that?" She turned her head and looked inquiringly at him.

"We can't have an affair. I am not able to." Peter looked away.

"Oh. Well, I suppose it's just as well."

"Just as well?"

"I don't like to poach on other women's men. I like to think that I'm above that sort of thing."

"Well, then. That settles it." Peter got up and stared down at her. He tried to study her face but he wasn't getting much from her expression. "You don't mind. We had a fling. That's all there is to it."

Rebecca stood up as well. "Yes, we had a fling.

I - There was a bombing. I wanted you to stay. You wanted to stay as well."

He closed his eyes and sighed. "No, we had a fling and I wanted you." He shook his head slightly. She gave him the right answer. Telling her that he wanted her would have lured him back to being her lover. "Alright. I must go. I hope you will forgive me."

"I forgive you. I will be fine. Certainly."

Peter walked to the door. He opened it and walked through it. He dared to look at her again before he closed it behind him.

Rebecca, alone, held herself and then she walked to her bedroom, the magazine forgotten on the couch.

Not long after, another rap on the door sounded. "It's me, Peter again. Let me in."

She gasped and ran to the door, opened it and then smiled at him radiantly. "Come in."

He saw her face and then he pulled her to him and kissed her long and hard. "Close the door." She murmured against his mouth. He obliged, then he pulled her to him again.

"I'm a sorry cad, my dear girl." He said softly. "I am so very dull at this. I've had a life that's been all about - " Peter paused. "Listen, I can't really tell you but your life is in danger because you and I are lovers. We have to pretend we're on the outs. Ok?"

Rebecca's face registered understanding but what she said was, "I'm not sure what you are. But you seem to be very troubled. Your job - it's all about that bombing, isn't it?"

He sighed with relief. "Yes. Now I am going to be back with you soon but you have to go on with life as usual. Go to work, do whatever you wish. Your parents are here, are they not?" Peter's eyes scanned her face to survey the emotions that passed through it.

"Yes, they're here. For a few weeks - maybe only two." Rebecca tugged at his lapel. "Peter, I'd like us to be together again. When will that happen?"

Peter's face was inscrutable. "I don't know. I have a lot of things to do - I might have to leave my job to devote to our affair. I can't do both."

"I see. If that's the case I think it might be too much for you. You need a job - I can always wait and we can find time somehow...". Rebecca's voice trailed, and Peter's heart was heavy as he regarded the slight downturn of the corners of her mouth.

"I can always find something else to do." He tried to sound encouraging. But the prospect of a staid life with Rebecca gave him pause.

She looked encouraged. "It will be ok, Peter. I'm willing to do what needs to be done. Go and do what you want to do."

Peter said nothing. He closed his eyes briefly and breathed in her soft perfume.

"I'm dangerous to you dear girl. That is what I wanted to tell you."

"I don't know what to say, Peter."

"I must have you - I don't now what I can do - I've been tormented by this."

She gazed up at him questioningly. "Do you think we - us - do our feelings have a happy future, Peter?"

"I don't know. I've been in this work forever, it seems. I feel almost as though this sort of thing - I've shelved it from my life for as long. I've been convinced, you see, that I could never have this with anyone. Then, I met you."

They stood in each other's arms for what seemed

an eternity. Rebecca's eyes filled with tears and she
strove to control them. It seemed too much to bear. He
felt her shoulders shake softly and then he groaned.
"I'm so very sorry, Rebecca."

They couldn't speak after that and finally, he let
her go. "We will be together soon. I have to go one with
this last job for them. Then I will - we will - be
together."

He held her from him and looked away from her
tear-streaked face.

"In the meantime, be with your parents during
your free time - I want you to always be with somebody.
And don't talk to Elena at all. Understood?"

"Understood".

"I have to go."

"It's alright. I will be fine. Do what you need to
do."

Peter's face became like a stone. He left her quickly and disappeared down the hall.

Chapter Nineteen

Rebecca awoke the next day to a brilliant sunshine streaming through her bedroom window. She stretched, yawned and then settled back in her pillow thinking about her evening last night. She remembered her parents' consternation with her statement that she wanted to stay in London. Her father's perspicacity when he said he wanted to give her time to think about it and whether this Peter Reed fellow was being honorable in his intentions.

Rebecca lingered over her interlude with Peter. A smile hovered over her lips and she closed her eyes. His kiss was so memorable and she felt a wish to bury her face in his shoulder. The only thing handy was her pillow but she didn't care.

The phone rang in the kitchen and burst her reverie.

Rebecca got up reluctantly and put on her slippers. It was almost six a.m.

When she got to the phone, it stopped. Rebecca ignored the intrusion and went about the business of preparing her breakfast. The phone rang again and this time, she answered it.

"Hello."

"Hi love, it's Elena. How are you?" Elena's smoky voice came to her ears. Rebecca recoiled from the sound, half guilty and half because she didn't much care of Elena.

"Hello Elena. I'm fine. How are you?"

Elena sounded amused, as though she knew about Rebecca's tryst with her fiancé. "I'm good. Very good. I'm wondering if you had thought of the house party that my friend Max is giving this weekend. I want you to come. It will give you a taste of English society."

Rebecca did not speak at first. Then she said, "I'm not sure yet Elena. I think it might be fun but my parents are in town."

"Oh. It might be that I can persuade my friend Max to accommodate another couple." Elena paused, breathlessly.

"I might ask my parents. They aren't really good with these things. Dad has never spent the weekend with strangers."

"Max is a lovely man. He wouldn't mind, really."

"Well, let me ask them."

"Yes, do that."

"Who is Max? I don't think you ever spoke of him." Rebecca spoke easily, leaning against the counter.

"Max is a good friend. I haven't told you much about him because Peter would mind."

"Oh. You mean Max is another lover of yours?"

"It's something people do in this country. Lovers are not uncommon."

"But Peter is your fiancé, Elena."

Elena said nothing then she sighed over the phone. "My dear Rebecca, you are such an innocent."

Rebecca frowned and then she smiled to herself. "I must be. Why don't I ask my parents and if they want to go then I will go too."

"Perfect. Call me when you've spoken to them alright?"

Rebecca hung up and sat down, nursing her coffee. Many thoughts went in and out of her head. She sighed and sipped her black coffee, trying to dispel the sound of Elena's voice from her mind.

Finally, she got up to make her cereal.

When Rebecca's mother arrived, she was surprised that Rebecca was not ready to leave. Sophia took in the messy living room and the unwashed dishes in the sink and then looked at her daughter's face. Rebecca seemed to be in a good mood, and her face - still unwashed - had a sheen to it. "Are you alright, Rebecca?" Asked Sophia.

"Oh, yes I am." Rebecca said sunnily.

Sophia said nothing at first. "Well, we should be

getting ready to go. What if you went and got ready and I'll see how I can get the apartment looking better, how's that?"

Rebecca's face flushed. "Oh, Mom!" She looked around as though she had not seen her flat at all that morning. She took in the dirty dishes, the mess in the living room - towels and magazines all awry. "I'm so sorry. I just felt as though I - "

"I what?"

"Oh, well, I'm feeling out of sorts - kind of - well," she stammered and then became quiet.

"Rebecca, are you feeling alright?" Sophia's eyes seemed to take in the light in Rebecca's face. "Are you pregnant?" Her words escaped her and Sophia felt shock at the sound and import of what she asked her daughter.

Rebecca said nothing and yet her shrug said it all.

"What happened? Who - Who's the father?" Sophia's face became white. She groped for a chair and sank into it.

"Oh, Mom. It's not that bad. I'm in love with him. He's so very good!" Rebecca said reassuringly.

Sophia passed a hand over her face. "Ok, well. You are sure you're pregnant?"

Rebecca replied slowly, "No, but I know I am. I have to go to get it confirmed."

"Do you know anyone here - an OB that can see you?"

"No, but the hospital has someone on staff, I'm sure." Rebecca said with some hesitation. It occurred to her that this news might make her situation somehow an unpleasant one. The thought came unbidden and yet it sounded as though it came from Peter's voice. "I'll figure it out, Mom. Now, let me get myself ready."

"Are you having symptoms? Something like tummy problems or what?"

"No not exactly. I'm ok. Really. I'll go find something in the closet and put it on and we can find a cab and get to that place we talked about last night, ok?"

"That's fine, dear. I'm going to help with tidying up, ok? I'm a little excited, dear. I think that might be good for your father and me."

Rebecca stopped in her tracks and turned around. "You'll have to tell Dad."

"Only if you want me to." Sophia said meekly.

"Well, let's wait a bit, ok? I've yet to tell the father." Rebecca smiled impishly and disappeared into her bedroom.

Sophia decided to fend off the warring thoughts in her mind about this news. It was shocking yet, but knowing that her daughter was a very pretty girl it wasn't a surprise. It seemed to Sophia that when her daughter and Cor eloped to England months ago, that it would have happened then. A little baby on the way. It happened everyday, didn't it? Sophia took a few of the magazines that lay on the sofa and love seat and folded them shut, placing them in a small stack on the side table. Then, after she did a few more decluttering motions, Sophia sat down and thought in earnest.

It was going to be something that would have to be discussed with Leo. Her breathing became rushed at the thought. She had to think, and think clearly, with purpose. What would happen if her daughter really were pregnant. Clearly the pregnancy was wanted. Her memory of her daughter looking so happy made it clear. Then what about her husband? Did he want to get back home so soon? They only had two weeks. She tried to think about canceling her flight back. Leo had to return so it was something that she had to make clear to him. Leo needed to understand. *I am needed here,* Sophia told herself firmly. She shifted uncomfortably in her seat. Well, it made her feel better that she would stay here while her daughter was going through her pregnancy. Oh, it made her sad to think of leaving her daughter now that she had to have her around. What would life be for a pregnant girl alone in a big and foreign city like London? Her mind whirled and made her feel ill.

Sophia got up and paced the floor. It was her decision, she thought. No, she didn't care if Rebecca didn't want her around. No, she won't cramp her at all. She can still be and do as she liked. If the man were a decent man, he would do all he could to take care his girl would be as comfortable as possible, and that she didn't have to suffer the difficulties of pregnancy. Who was this man, Sophia asked. She didn't know who any of Rebecca's friends were in this London. Sophia walked to her daughter's kitchen and saw Rebecca's cellphone on the counter.

Sophia felt a tickle of fear in her gut. It was too rude. No, it was rude. But she wanted to find out. She heard the shower in the bathroom turn on. Quickly, Sophia went to the cell phone and looked at it. She saw it had a PIN to enter. She guessed at a PIN and got into it easily. The cell phone had texts and she saw Peter's text to Rebecca this morning. It was too telling to read it but she saw the first few words. It was enough to tell her this was the father of her grandchild.

Peter. Sophia put down the phone and smiled in triumph. It was not a problem now to figure out who he was. She saw his name and then something occurred to her. A niggling thought. This man would be too much to deal with at this time.

Sophia walked away and went to the living room. Her thoughts went back and forth. She didn't see his last name. It had to be someone from work, she thought. Finally, with a sigh, Sophia decided it was a better idea to break the news to Leo that she wanted to stay on and not go back to Connecticut.

Chapter Twenty

Mother and daughter ventured out into the sunlight and hailed a cab to bring them to *Arabella's* near Regent Street where they would take their lunch. Sophia, delighted at the sunny weather, commented, "We've had the best luck here this visit. I'm expecting that the rains would start up at any time. Have you always been this lucky, Rebecca?"

Her daughter, intent on following the direction

that the cab was taking, answered, "Mom, it's had its

share of rain and fog. But fog has not been that bad.

Some of my coworkers say that the fog has not been

thick as before due to the way the temperatures have

been off the water." She leaned back in the cab, satisfied

that they were headed the right way. "Sorry I was

distracted, Mom. I don't always know what route the

taxi takes when I use the service. I like to take the bus

and it gives me a lot more freedom to see what the lay of

the land looks like here."

"I see. Well, I'm all excited. I love London. I

met your father here a long time ago, when I was here

for my sixteenth birthday. Your grandparents and I were

here for a long vacation. That was when life was so

much happier for our family."

"I know you took a good number of pictures - I

remember you put them in a photo album at home."

"Do you? Yes, it's at home in the library."
Sophia surveyed the traffic around Regent Street where
the overhanging banners of the British flag cheered them
as they drove past. "Such a very exhilarating view. I
can understand why you love this new city of yours,
Rebecca." Her face seemed to take on a thoughtful
aspect. "Dear daughter, you don't miss Connecticut
anymore?"

Rebecca shook her head. "I've had a taste of
London and it's very much in my system. I am very
much interested in it, its ups and downs, but mainly
because I've made a good living her so far."

"And what about Cor?"

"Oh, Cor." Rebecca shrugged. "He was a
disappointment."

"And yet London isn't?"

"I fell in love with London. My infatuation with

Cor - it was so hard to see that he wasn't for me. Mom, he had a lot of problems and he hid them well. I didn't see how it was like until he was away from his friends. Away from his enablers. People like Mike Oates, who handled his debts for him. People like that."

Sophia nodded. "Ok, so now what? What will be your future now? What plans are you making?"

There was a long pause. Rebecca's face was averted and she watched the shoppers on the sidewalk. The cab swerved to enter Sloan Street and the beautiful storefronts greeted them. Sophia glanced at them and yet she waited for her daughter to answer.

"I am still thinking what to do. I do have my flat. I have my job at the hospital. I'm fine with money. I don't have a car and I don't need it here." Rebecca replied finally. She didn't mention that she felt impeded in mentioning Peter. Peter seemed to be a topic she shied away from with her mother.

Sophia took this reticence in stride. There would be enough opportunity to discuss this pregnancy. The very word still shocked Sophia. Looking at her daughter's profile, Sophia experienced a pang of worry and sadness. It was so difficult to bridge the time where they had first said farewell and this time that they had together. The gap in time made it hard for her to approach her daughter and take up where they left off. Rebecca was another person now, tinged with a patina of worldliness in a city of worldly people.

"I see our restaurant now." Rebecca leaned forward and asked the cab driver to stop at the earliest opportunity.

The cab slowed down and then stopped. Both of the passengers alighted. After paying the cab driver, Rebecca straightened up and walked a few steps to her mother who had walked a bit away to look at a shop window. The window displayed the very British products of woolen and cashmere dresses and scarves. "Lovely!" Exclaimed Sophia. She longed to go inside and take a look.

"Would you like to browse inside?" Rebecca asked, eager as well to check the place out. "I'm told that the Duchess of Cambridge shops here regularly.

"Oh!"

"I think they're very expensive. It might be almost like browsing a museum for what they display. Look and admire but don't think of buying." A chuckle escaped Rebecca's lips as they lingered outside the door.

"Oh let's check it out later. I need to eat something." Sophia turned away. "Maybe after a good English lunch we can go and walk it off. The weather is much too good to waste on cabs. I am wearing sensible shoes as well, so let's go find us some grub, shall we?

Laughing, they both walked quickly to cross the street and came to the assigned restaurant which opened its doors to both of them, a smiling concierge inviting them inside.

Chapter Twenty-One

Leo looked across the room full of surgeons and smiled

to himself. He enjoyed this and relished the back and

forth with these intelligent men and, yes, women, who

thought of his presentation and asked good questions.

Leo Bartholomew knew from experience that it was the

bane of his existence. Practicing surgery was good, it

was exhilarating because he was like God, somehow.

His hands made the hurt go away. It made him feel

exultant when the patient went home and made strides in their recovery. Leo did not lose patients frequently. His batting average was good. It made him famous. Many people asked him to give his wisdom to others. They promoted him with alacrity where he worked. Many other renowned centers of heart surgery asked him to work for them. He resisted. At times, he felt the pull. But he enjoyed living in Connecticut. In the tree lined street where his house of 34 years stood, surrounded by similar houses, well built, somewhat old fashioned, a bit above the usual type of Connecticut homes. A rich neighborhood. Where his wife and daughter enjoyed all the comforts.

The question and answer started. Leo fielded the questions with ease. It was like having them eating out of his hand. It made his day and he felt a lift in his heart. This was the life. He enjoyed himself, made his struggle feel like it was nothing. His hating the traveling and all that dragging of luggage, the hoisting of winter coats or other accessories made it a drudge and yet here he was, admired by English surgeons. No, not just English surgeons. British surgeons. The Royal College of Surgeons, to be exact.

Out of the corner of his eye, he espied a man in a Mackintosh enter the room. Leo recognized him and he didn't bat an eyelash. He continued with the discussion. The man took a chair in the back and nodded imperceptibly. Something in his demeanor gave Leo pause. He actually coughed, which he rarely did in his talks.

Finally, the moderator rose from his chair next to him. "Dr Bartholomew, we thank you for spending your valuable time with us and traveling all the way from Connecticut to be with us."

"Thank you Sir Hughes." Leo smiled and shook hands. It was his cue that his performance was over. As if to confirm, the audience clapped hands.

Sir Hughes, a tall and distinguished man in his sixties, nodded at the audience. "Let's have a break, shall we? We can meet again in - " he consulted his pocket watch. "How about twenty minutes?"

Everyone seemed to agree and there was a general shuffling of chairs, and murmurs. The crowd got up severally and made a queue to the doors. The program had been for the day. Leo's presentation was the first one up and there would be a few more less important talks of the day.

Sir Hughes turned to Leo. "Leo, excellent talk. I'm sure everyone will be eager to discuss with you at the reception later about how the techniques you describe are like. The usual things - you know what I mean." He paused. "I'm hoping we could chat later afterwards. You were interested in a topic which I might be able to help you with. You are possibly thinking of spending more time in England is that what you thought?"

Leo cleared his throat. "Well, yes. I'm here not only to be with you and the RCS but I'm actually visiting my only child. She's here working in London."

"Is that so?" Hughes asked, his bushy eyebrows lifting.

"Oh yes. She's actually working in one of the hospitals here. Charing Cross."

"Charing Cross." Repeated Sir Hughes.

"So," Leo said slowly. "I'm thinking of retiring from work in the US and possibly working here - or perhaps, being of a different function here. Perhaps you and I might explore that possibility?"

Sir Hughes nodded, as though he got the gist of his intent. 'Well, my dear Leo, we would be glad to have you as someone who's a leading expert in this area. I suspect many places here would give their eye teeth to have you on their staff. That is," he paused, "if you weren't actually retiring? Which is it to be?"

Leo stood back on his heels. "I'm a bit torn. Let's say I stay here for the few weeks or a few months to see what I could get into, ostensibly looking for a place to live and retire, then when it's time and people are used to seeing me and having me as a visiting surgeon - is that possible?"

Hughes smiled finally, and Leo read this as acceptance. Leo felt relief surge through his mind.

"Yes, of course. That might be the thing to do." He ushered Leo to the door where outside some coffee, tea and sweets were on display. 'Why don't you and I talk again later and then we can help you with finding a good man to help with finding a place to stay for - say - a few months, before you finally have your family sink roots in the place?"

"Yes, sounds good. Thank you, Sir Hughes."

They wandered out to the hallway and looked through the display on the long and cloth covered table which groaned with all the delicacies that the English were famous for.

As they passed, the man in the Mackintosh looked at Leo who ignored him. He heard them discuss Leo's plans to set household in London. A slight frown clouded the man's face. He turned away and took out his cell phone.

"Made contact but he's not yet talked to me." He tapped out the words.

After some seconds, the response came back: "Get him to meet you. It's important."

The Mackintosh man spelled out his reply. "He isn't his usual friendly self."

"He can't reveal himself. Just blend in. If it takes too long, wait for him somewhere else."

Damn. The man in the Mackintosh hated having to tail people. "Ok. Text later,"

The day stretched long and the man in the Mackintosh began to feel lost in the discussions, Nobody seemed to notice him, save for the usher who came to him and asked him if he signed his name on the roster. He looked at her in surprise, then he went over to the roster on the table near the door. He wrote the name "Doctor Rupert Ashworth, Leeds Hospital"

Once he had got back to his chair, the usher smiled at him brightly and left him alone.

Leo finally said his goodbyes and promised the ones who hung about him to keep in touch. Many invited him to visit their hospitals and go through their Grand Rounds with them. Leo was touched and happy. "Yes, I'll come by. Tomorrow? Yes, what time? Ok, that's fine. I'll look for you. Yes oh you'll be expecting me? Good, that's great. See you then! Yes, of course. I'll come by. Yes. Ok, thanks!"

They all waved at him and then he was leaving. He went towards the first floor elevators and got in. While he was in it he saw the Mackintosh man. Leo lost his smile and stood expecting something.

"You're a hard man to pin down, Leo."

"What do you want?"

"I need you to talk to someone. He is eager to talk."

"Where?"

"What about going to the London Eye? Here's a ticket." He handed him the ticket to get into a bin. "Someone there will be your contact. Go there tomorrow at 3 pm."

"Fine." Leo pocketed the ticket and when the doors opened, he left quickly.

Chapter Twenty-Two

The conversation and shopping with Sophia was great

fun for Sophia but Rebecca found it intolerable. She had

to think and she couldn't. Her insides were feeling out

of sorts. How long she was pregnant was on her mind.

She felt unsure and wanted to talk to Peter. Yet he

hadn't texted her nor did he call. Not at all. She felt

alone and yet somewhat connected to him.

Sophia, who was fondling a lovely cashmere

sweater, glanced at her daughter. "Nice color, dear. What do you think? Should I buy it?"

"Oh," Rebecca looked at it and tried to act as though she was interested. "Oh, yes. Fine."

"I think you should buy a lot of things for your work wardrobe. Do you have to wear a lab coat?"

"No. No lab coat," Rebecca replied offhandedly.

"Oh, well then you will definitely love nice tops like these. And try to display your lovely legs, Those will definitely make those nice English men take note,"

Rebecca tried to laugh. "Oh Mom."

"Well you - " she faltered remembering that her daughter was pregnant. 'I'm sorry. You already have a man. You need to tell me about him."

Her daughter stepped away and tried to look at another piece of clothing. "Mom, I am not sure I can."

"Oh? Is he already taken?"

Her daughter's sigh made Sophia feel the worst. "He's engaged to someone else."

"Oh Rebecca!"

Rebecca shook her head. "We had a one night stand."

Someone who was also in the vicinity heard her and gazed at the both with a look. Sophia took her daughter aside. She hissed, "Rebecca, what on earth do you mean by going with a man who's already taken? I have told you time and again never to poach. What on earth did you do? Did you mean to seduce him?" There was fire in Sophia's eyes as she interrogated her daughter, "I'm really disappointed in you. You leave home eloping with Cor the next thing you're pregnant with some other man's baby!"

Rebecca stood unbowed and listened to her mother. "Mother I am not so bad as that, I happened to like this guy and he was so handsome and well mannered and - "

"Is that what I taught you to like off the bat? Can't believe this. A handsome man. A man who's well mannered. Ohhh, I am not happy at all with you." Sophia shook her dark head sadly, forgetting the clothes they were shopping for.

"Well, here it is Mom. I am in love with him.. And I'm carrying his baby."

"Are you really in love? And are you really pregnant? Have you seen anyone about this?"

"No, I mean I know I'm pregnant. I missed my period. I never miss it. And I will find one of this gadgets that show I'm pregnant."

"And what of this guy? How long have you known this guy? You say he's engaged. Is this engagement with a decent woman? Oh, this is such a bad idea. You might have to leave and have the baby in the States. We will take care of this." Her mother decidedly said. Sophia started to walk purposefully towards the door.

Rebecca whirled around, her face mutinous. "NO! I am old enough Mom. I am in love with Peter and once he gets out of his relationship he and I will be a couple and we'll get married."

"Listen to yourself. You are like an accident that everyone wants to gawk at. Oh my god. What will I tell your father?"

Rebecca left her side and went in search of another spot in the store to stand next to. She wasn't in tears yet but she was angry. She wanted to believe that Peter loved her and would make it alright soon.

Sophia came to her side. "Alright, Rebecca. You are a grown adult. I can't say that you've been the most well behaved woman in the world. You are someone who goes from one guy to another and found this guy you thought you could love. He isn't good and now I am not sure that this Peter person is any better. Does he even have a job? Can he support you? What does he say?" She became alarmed. "Did you tell him yet?"

"Look Mom, I will take care of it. Don't get all ballistic about it. I'll take care of everything."

"What if he doesn't want the baby?"

"I think he will." Rebecca's voice faltered.

"I think he might just become a stranger, that's what I think." Sophia took a shirt from a hanger and absently caressed the material. "I'm not sure we can talk this way here. We're already getting stares from the shoppers."

"Let me take you to the area where they have tea here. We can have some of their famous sweets."

Rebecca said helplessly. "I have to sit down."

"What are you feeling?"

"I'm feeling like needing a chair. I am feeling pretty darn upset and your questions are making me feel sick. So, if you don't mind, I want to go where I can have some food and some coffee and then we can sit in silence. I don't want anymore of this twenty questions."

Sophia stood helplessly for a minute and then scanned the store for any signs that a cafe might be in the area. "Here, come with me. I'm sorry dear, but I can't believe this is happening to my girl. You are a terrible girl to subject me to this problem. I'm not supposed to be staying here for long. I will be so worried about you when we're back in the States."

Rebecca had a few words in mind to say about that but her common sense told her to keep herself quiet.

The table the chose to sit in was in a quiet alcove of the store cafe and their waiter came to get their order. "I'll have some coffee and one of your lovely scones please," spoke Sophia.

"Would you like a bit of clotted cream and jam?" Asked the waiter,

"Please."

Rebecca said she wanted the same thing and then she took out her cell phone. She stared at it and saw nothing that showed her that Peter texted.

They sat and waited for their food. Neither wanted to speak first. Then Sophia's cell phone rang and both women sighed in relief. "It's your father," Sophia said. "Hello? Hi. It's really gotten too late, has it? Well we're shopping at Harrods. Yes. Very nice. Very expensive, You think I can buy something? Good dear, I will. But I'm with Rebecca. She's fine," she glanced at Rebecca. "Oh, is that right? Tomorrow? We haven't planned. You're seeing some of the surgeons' hospitals. Oh, just like old times. Fine. I'll find something to do. Yes."

She leaned over to Rebecca. "Are you back to work tomorrow?"

"Yes."

"Leo? She's back to work tomorrow. Fine. We'll eat somewhere later. Anything here in town you recommend, Rebecca?"

"I don't know. I'd ask the front desk."

"Leo? Let's ask the front desk. Yes, Fine. Goodbye,"

Rebecca had her speech prepared by the time her mother hung up on her father. "Look, Mom. I know that I've been a bit of a trial for you and Dad. I was a girl who had all that I ever wanted thanks to you both. Now I want to live my life as a responsible adult here in this lovely and vibrant city. I've fallen in love with it. At least, I thought I fell in love with it. But I've got no friends except perhaps Peter. I guess he was so decent and felt as though he was interested in me. When that bomb went off close to where I had my place he stayed and gave me some company. Then things got a bit hot and we made love."

Sophia looked at her with sympathy. "Oh, Rebecca."

"He was so very good at making me feel good so very good that I fell for him instantly. He had already seen me a few times before and each time I felt something like a pull between us. I think he felt the same thing. I know he's engaged but the woman isn't a good one for him. She's selfish and self-absorbed. I suspect she's seeing someone also."

"So did he say he was going to break it off with her?"

"I don't know that he said it in so many words."

"Oh, my dear girl," her mother exclaimed.

"I am a mess but I know he's the one I want. I don't know what will happen. He told me he wanted to keep seeing me, but he wants to pretend we're on the outs."

"Pretend?' Sophia looked surprised.

"Well, I think it is so the other woman doesn't get suspicious. I think he wants to work things out so it will be good when we're together."

Sophia looked sharply at her. "Do you know this for a fact or are you imagining this as what you think it ought to be? Rebecca you really have to talk to someone about this,"

The vision of the psychiatrist came to Rebecca's mind. She ignored this and instead said. "I'll take about it - but maybe not yet, I won't say anything to Peter right now. I'm not sure he wants to have this complication."

"And so you'll go and be an unwed woman without a man to take care of you? In London," Sophia picked up her spoon and played with it with a lackluster movement. "You have to be sure you want to go through this pregnancy."

"I do. I don't want to give this baby up."

"Ok, fine. I'm glad you said that. Now, I am not sure but your father will have to find out."

"Don't tell him yet."

"I don't want to delay."

"Mom, please don't tell him," Rebecca said pleadingly. "Make Dad think things are all normal.

You'll be gone in a couple of weeks. I'll keep you both posted."

"No, we won't be gone for good. Your Dad wants us to retire here someday."

Rebecca paused in surprise.

"Yes. Dear daughter we miss you and we want to see you often. You being pregnant is another confirmation we have to stay here. You shouldn't be worried. We will be here for you. No matter what."

Rebecca's chest lifted and fell. A surprising sense of relief came over her. "Mom, I am glad. I know that I could do this without you but now that you've said this, I'm real glad."

They linked hands across the table and settled down to eat in silence.

Chapter Twenty-Three

Leo stepped out of his cab and walked to the landmark
called the London Eye. He had not been to this landmark
before in his previous travels to London. He looked at it
with suspicion - he thought it was a glorified Ferris
wheel but when he came closer to it he saw that the
'bins' or 'cabs' that were stationed all over the wheel
that turned were big enough to accommodate a group of
passengers.

He went to the kiosk where they were collecting tickets and handed his to the man. "Hullo Sir. We'll be moving in a few minutes. Step into the bin that's level with the ground. You'll see the door is open and there's a space to move around in. Don't do a lot of moving though Keep from being jostled. Don't do any jumping or running in place. Just enjoy the view. We move a bit slowly so don't get too impatient. You might like to get a bottle of water but we don't want you to wish for the loo and make a problem for yourself."

"Fine."

He moved away and went to the bin that was gaping open. There wasn't anyone there at the time he approached but as he stepped inside, a man came in with him. "Hi," The man looked at him. "Leo Bartholomew?"

"Yes."

The man was well dressed, but not out of the ordinary. He was a tall man, a few inches taller than Leo. He also had an American accent.

"Why don't we change our minds and get out of here, Leo?"

Leo looked relieved. "I wasn't interested in taking this thing anyway."

The man led him out and then they walked along the river in silence. Leo looked around with some interest. A nice enough day. It was a bit overcast and there was a chill wind from the water's edge.

"I'm sure you know why we are here together." Said the man.

"Do you have a name?"

"Call me Chuck."

"Alright, Chuck. What are we here for?"

"You know that you've been asked before to help us with some information exchange,"

"Yes. And I wish to make this the last one."

"You'll have to discuss it with the man upstairs."

"Is it still Perkins?"

"I don't know. I'm reporting to someone else they might know each other."

"Oh. Well alright."

"What do you have for me now?"

Leo took out a plain white envelope and let Chuck see it. "Ok?"

"Ok." Chuck said coolly. "Don't give it to me. Someone else will pick it up. Just pass by that trash bin a few feet down and drop it inside. Then walk away and never look back."

"Ok.'

"That's all. I'll say goodbye. I won't say anymore about us."

Leo felt a tightening of his necktie and walked away from Chuck. He walked leisurely to the trash bin and then he dropped the envelope inside. He moved away quickly and when he reached the curb took the first bus and went inside.

A few yards away, a man in a red Man UTD jacket walked to the trashbin and took out the envelope. Unbenknownst to him, a man in a cab was watching. He had a high speed camera focused on the trash bin and once the Man UTD-jacketed man left the man in the cab tapped the cab driver and told him to leave.

Another cab peeled away before his and followed

the bus that Leo Bartholomew was riding in.

Chapter Twenty-Four

The night clubs were in full swing around the Baker Street address where Moorhead and Margo hunkered over their laptops. "Seems that our operation might be in some trouble, Margo my girl." Spoke Moorhead as he peered over his laptop to smile briefly at Margo.

She looked up, her glossy and dark hair swinging slightly with the movement of her head. "Oh" she shrugged. "What else is new?"

"Our man Peter's turned in his gun."

"Oh, that's old hat. What more do you know?"

"You listened!" Moorhead hissed, shocked. "Girl, you can't listen before I do."

"So give me a spanking." She stuck her tongue out at him. "I apologize. Watkins secretary was all agog with the news."

"Let's hope she didn't tell the rest of the neighborhood of Chelsea."

"No, I'm sure she didn't."

"Well, now you might guess that one girl named Rebecca Bartholomew is preggo?"

Margo's smile widened. "Oho. Good for my man Peter. He's had it coming."

"You think he'd just cavalierly inseminate a non-operative with this his stuff?"

"No, I guess he'd got himself so strung out or something. Maybe he was three fifths drunk?"

"I don't know but it was not a good move."

"Well, he's resigned. He can do what he wants with whomever he wants."

Moorhead shrugged. "I'm afraid he will be a very sad man. A kid on the way. The others will shun him."

"No baby showers for the man of the moment." Margo chuckled.

"I feel sorry for him."

The door opened suddenly and Peter entered, looking as smooth as ever. The others gawked at him.

Moorhead sputtered. "You - You - "

"Yes, it's me." Peter smiled thinly.

"What are you doing here?" Asked Margo.

"I'm here because I miss you both. Especially

Moorhead." He went over and chuffed Moorhead's reddish brown hair.

"Seriously you're supposed to be officially out of the force."

"I am but I'm sure that is going to be marked as being out of it officially but still having my hand in."

"Ok. So you're still in the operation. Are you still our man in charge?"

"No."

"Who is it then?"

"Tell me who Watkins asked after I left." Peter said, his arms folded as he leaned next to Moorhead's desk.

"Watkins called Perkins."

"The CIA man." Margo volunteered.

"I see. Well we have a few things on that man, do we not?"

"He's a shit." Moorhead said evenly.

"And I'm on his tail. It will be fine. I'll let Perkins do what he thinks he can do. In the meantime, I want to ask you all about this Bartholomew doctor."

"What?" Moorhead asked.

"Don't you have a dossier on him?"

"I do."

"Tell me about it."

"He's a famous heart surgeon. Travels to give lectures. He's here for one of them."

"And?"

"Better tell him, Moorhead." Margo said with a resigned tone.

Moorhead sat back, sighing. "Some fellow came to him at the conference and handed him something. Then after that we followed Bartholomew. He went to the London Eye Before he got himself inside it, another man in a Man United jacket asked him to leave and then they walked a bit. Bartholomew handed over a sheaf of papers in an unmarked envelope."

"Crap." Peter said with feeling. He turned and stood apart for a moment. Somehow it made it harder for him to get his thoughts in order. Somehow it made it hard for him to think of Rebecca.

"Sorry Peter." Margo said looking helpless. "We know she was a good girl - at least you thought she was."

Moorhead shot Margo a warning look. "I don't think the daughter knows about her father."

"Where did the envelope end up?" Asked Peter, his voice sounding hollow.

"We think it went to Perkin's desk."

"Ah I see."

"If you need to talk about it - "

"Well, I can't talk about it."

"You're officially out of the force. Go and talk about it with me. I want to tell you something else."

"Christ, what else do you know you bugger?" Peter asked with a reddened face. He sat down and looked intently at Moorhead.

"Ok, here goes." Moorhead stood up and paced the floor. Finally, he said, "Rebecca thinks she's preggo."

Peter laughed and then paused. Then he laughed. It was a mirthless laugh. But then he ended up with a smile on his face. "I'm dashed if I am going to be a father." He stopped suddenly. "It couldn't be anyone else's would it?"

"Well, we haven't any genetic means to tell but for all we can tell it's your kid."

"If she is really pregnant."

Peter sighed. "That complicates matters."

"Yes." The two chorused.

"I guess I might have to do something about this."

"What will you do?" Moorhead asked. "Just in case this happens to me. Just on the off chance." He shrugged, looking slightly bemused.

"I don't want to even think about what you ought to do."

"Will you tell her to get rid of it?" Margo asked.

"No."

"Then she's going to have to go with that Corcoran. He'll forgive her. He will, I'm sure."

Peter looked at him as though he was about to hit him. "No, not at all. This kid is mine. I've no real recollection what they told us when we were going through training at MI5. Babies weren't the big topic at the time. No. I will have to figure out what I need to do. She's still here. Her parents are here. Her father's probably a spook. And I don't like that at all."

"Then we will see about sending you and Rebecca a little card with a stork on the cover." Margo giggled.

"No don't do that."

"You will tell her you know?"

"Mmm." Peter was not sure he wanted to talk about it. "I'll see." He got up and headed to the door. "I shouldn't tell Watkins and don't tell about Rebecca's condition, ok?"

"Sure."

"And this weekend party. Go try to see what we can get from the watchers ok? And don't tell Perkins anything."

"Can we tell Perkins about Bartholomew?"

"No. Perkins needs to be happy we don't know about Bartholomew."

With those words, Peter left.

Chapter Twenty-Five

Leo arrived at their hotel sometime after five thirty p.m.

He looked as though he had been in high wind, his hair

(what was left of it) was tousled. He did not try to get it

to rights. He rushed into the hotel lobby, not noticing

the man at the desk who glanced up and then tried not to

look at him too closely.

Leo made his way into the nearest elevator and

got in. A few other people came inside as well. A

couple was having an argument and from their accents they sounded American. Leo closed his eyes and bided his time as the floors came and went.

"Look Elise, it's really time for you to come to terms about this tour. I really can't stand having to look for you at every turn. I'm so fucking tired of it and I want you to stand by and watch where everyone is headed to. Do you understand?" The man in the Burberry scarf, looking every inch the well fed American and sporting a sports jersey that declaimed "JETS" on it, stood beside Leo, but kept his focus on his girlfriend, who was in a high fashion coat from the same brand of Burberry. She looked down at her manicured hands in an attempt to find the words to tell her companion.

"Bill, I was only being a tourist. So why don't you just sit on it, ok?" She said with a primness that belied her very obviously well shod appearance.

"Ok, fine. If you get lost, Missy, I'll not look for you. Get it?"

She made a sound and turned away, which was at the direction of Leo, who looked even more uncomfortable.

Finally the elevator stopped and the arguing couple left.

Leo wiped his brow and looked around. He was with one more passenger, someone in a trilby hat and umbrella.

His floor was coming up, and then it was here. Leo stepped out and walked out to the hallway where he hurried to his room. He hoped that Sophia had not yet arrived.

Sophia, unknowing of Leo's impending arrival, was busy putting on her makeup in the bathroom. The music from the radio station abruptly stopped. A very determined voice of the announcer spoke: "We bring you the latest news. A new terrorist bomb has been defused in the are of High Street today at 5 p.m. The New Scotland Yard has informed Newscast that the area has been cleared, the bomb noticed by an alert passerby and bomb defusing teams worked to have it neutralized. There will be more news in the six o'clock hour. Stay tuned."

"My, what a relief!" Uttered Sophia as she paused to listen. She tried to shake off the feeling that came over her that danger was virtually everywhere in London. She decided to go to the cell phone she had on the desk and check up on Rebecca.

Rebecca was not home or was not answering it.

Sophia sighed and stood immobilized. It made her all the more worried. *Where was Leo?* She asked herself.

There was a sound of the door unlocking. Leo came through the door but he looked very strange.

"Hi, Leo, how was your day?" Sophia asked.

He said nothing and then he fell forward to the floor, face down. A knife was sticking out from his back.

Sophia uttered a scream and she screamed incessantly, her eyes horrified at the sight of her husband on the carpeted floor.

Sophia walked backwards unseeingly, and her outstretched hand found the telephone to the front desk.

"Hotel lobby, may I help you?" The voice answered.

"There's a - I mean, my husband. He's got something wrong. I think he's dead."

"Oh." There was a pause. "What room are you in?"

"Six nine nine."

"We'll get the police."

"Call an ambulance." Sophia spoke, a bit more herself. "I think he's still alive."

"Fine. We'll get there soon." The phone clicked and she was again by herself.

She tried not to look at Leo. She didn't want to touch him for some odd reason. It made her even more anguished. This was her husband of thirty years. It was so very difficult to go to his side and it made her eyes water. The deluge came and she sobbed loudly. It was all going wrong, she thought. It would have been so good to spend this day with him. Why did she not go and watch him talk at the College of Surgeons? Sophia hated London that moment. It made it all so bad, she said to herself.

The cell rang and Sophia went to pick it up. "Mom? It's me. Did you call?" Rebecca's voice came on the line,

"Yes, I did." Sophia said trying to control herself. "You need to come here soon as possible. Dad's gotten - " She couldn't speak. She started to cry again this time quietly, softly.

"Mom!" Rebecca sounded alarmed. "I'll be there as soon as I can."

Rebecca found her mother with several official looking

people. Her father's body was being taken away in a stretcher by medical personnel. There was a sudden fear that wrung Rebecca's insides as she watched this horrible tableau. "Oh my God." She uttered to herself. Visions of the future days ahead swam before her and she almost lost her footing as she walked to her mother's side.

"Are you the daughter?" A man in police uniform asked her suddenly.

"Yes. I'm Rebecca Bartholomew."

"Right. I'm Officer Dibble." He dug into his pocket and started a new page on his notebook.

"Is he going to be alright?"

He looked uncertain. "Let's say he's still got a sliver of life in his body. I won't predict anything - I'm not the medico." He went back to write on his notebook. "Your mother's been very very upset. They've had to give her a sedative. She's in the bedroom. We hope you could give us information."

"I'm a little bit unsteady. I'm ready to help but I'd like to go somewhere else. I think I could need some help, too. I -" She looked at him and he saw her looking very very much like what her mother looked like earlier.

"God, you look bad too. It's terribly sad. I'll fetch one of the women officers and she'll talk to you - take you to a better location."

"Thanks." She stood still while he got a female officer and she came along with him.

"Hi, I'm Officer Lane. You look like you need a sedative as well."

"No - I mean, not a sedative. Something not a drug please."

"Oh?" Officer Lane looked at her questioningly.

"I think I might be - pregnant."

Officer Lane exchanged glances with Officer Dibble.

"Well, we'll find something that's not - er - problematic." Officer Lane shepherded her to an empty room and there they talked in a quiet tone.

Dibble went to his superior, who was watching the crime scene experts. "Looks like the daughter's worse off than the Mum, Inspector Glade. I think she's also pregnant. "

"God that would make it seem so much worse. They're tourists, I take it."

"Well yes. American."

"We haven't seen anyone on this floor. The blood did not drip on his way from the lift. I think he might just die - such bad luck for this family."

They looked sadly at each other. Inspector Glade

closed the door behind them.

Chapter Twenty-Six

The news of Leo Bartholomew's attempt on his life reached Watkins as he sat in his office. The man who delivered the news was Moorhead, and they looked glumly at each other.

"I'm not sure if this has any bearing on anything, Moorhead."

"No, but I do know that Leo has been passing something to a man who works for one of our allies."

Watkins looked up. "Who?"

"I don't know yet. I think it's too soon to surmise."

"You know and yet you won't tell. Come on, Moorhead, tell me."

"I hate to surmise but I have a guess it's Perkins."

"And how do you come to this guess?"

"I have the video of the drop. I read his lips. He mentioned Perkins. The other man's name is Chuck."

"Damn."

"Yes, damn." Peter Reed entered at the same time Watkins uttered the oath.

"What are you doing here? You're gone. Taken a long retirement. What are you doing here?"

"I'm dashed if I know. All I know is that the man who's the father of the girl I love is dying at this moment in hospital. I need to make sure he gets out alive and goes back to America in one piece. And not in a box."

"Oh hell." Moorhead turned away with a smile in his face. "Reed, you are something else. Love doesn't count in these types of discussions. You know that don't you?"

"Go to hell Moorhead." Peter went to Watkins. His face looked grim.

"Oh what hell are we going to get into, Peter? What do you wish to do now? I am somewhat unable to grasp what it is you are up to as you don't damn well tell me. Tell me now."

"I'm not sure why Bartholomew has been picked as a passer of documents. I don't see him appearing in other visits to London - he's got a stellar background - "

"More the type we all like. You know that."

Moorhead said gravely.

"Oh hell." Watkins sat back and pushed off his desk. He got up and stood still, looking at Peter up and down.

"I'm thinking this guy Perkins is what we ought to focus on, Watkins. I think we need to watch who he's dealing with. I know he's eager to know all about that damned bastard - I forgot who they call him - oh, Revenor. I've been gone too long."

"Obviously." Watkins said with a smirk. "How is the girl you love doing? Is she protected? I don't want another member of the family getting into bad business. You attract that Peter. You do."

"I'm - hell, I know I do but I do love her and now I'm going to make damn sure she gets out of this city before things get worse."

"I - ah - think she has been watched since you

mentioned her," Moorhead said.

Peter looked at Moorhead coldly. "Yes, I know. I made that happen. I don't wish to do more now. I think you both know enough about Perkins. I'll make my own plans with Rebecca."

"Yes, do that." Watkins spat out. "You aren't wanted anymore. Just get that family out of here. We aren't into rescuing tourists as a rule."

"You're such a kind man." Peter said under his breath. He looked at Moorhead meaningfully before he left.

Moorhead put his hand over his face and looked away.

'You need to tell me what else is happening with him and that woman he loves." Watkins said to his underling with a grim face.

"She's his girl and he wants to have a life with

her. That's all. Isn't that acceptable to you?"

"Don't try to soften up, Moorhead. It's not going to be easy for you you know that."

"Well, fine. I won't say anymore about them. They're on their own."

"That's right."

"What about Perkins?"

"He's going to have to be taken care of. I'll speak to someone in the - the department of waste."

Moorhead looked at him with surprise, then he opened his mouth and then he closed it.

Peter waited until Moorhead left Watkins' office. He went in silently and then once he got to Watkins' door he stepped in. Watkins was busy reading a report and did not hear Peter enter. Then he realized there was someone else there and he looked up, swallowing hard and then gave a sigh of relief. "Oh God, you came back. Whatever for?"

"I need help, Watkins." Peter said simply. "I'm very concerned that my leaving MI5 will be the topic of conversation especially because everyone might know of my romance with Ms Bartholomew."

"So, that is true, but I'll try to keep it under wraps."

"I also want your help. We will need a new pair of passports and she and I need to have an exit that will make it quite clear that we are both no more in this world."

Watkins stared at him for a moment, then he relaxed. "Yes, I understand. We can help."

"I'll be most indebted to you, Watkins."

"You aren't really in the agency, Reed. You work for me, and not for them. As that role still exists but only because now you're being a nice enough fellow to hang about, we won't need too much of an exit strategy."

"I do think we need a good one. Mr Leo Bartholomew's background is suspect. I don't wish anyone of those spooks thinking that his daughter - attached to me - will be another spook in the making."

"Alright. We can stage a happening. An event. We can and have done so in the past for those who are in true danger of getting into a bad end with those who have crossed swords with them in the past."

"You get my meaning then."

"Alright," said Watkins again. He sighed and rubbed his forehead. "I'm getting a bit stressed thinking about it. I'll see what we can do. I won't say more. I'll have to think about it perhaps see how our close friend in Leeds will help in some way. Also, we might plant a story in the BBC newsreel. They're always very good about cooperating. We'll say it's a security matter. How's that?"

"Excellent." Peter drummed his fist on the table and then turned to leave. Then, he looked back at Watkins. "Very happy, Watkins."

His former superior smiled wanly at him and waved him away.

Chapter Twenty-Seven

Peter Reed took the fastest route to the hospital. In his mind, the death - or impending death - of Leo Bartholomew was all going too fast. His own preference was to make things easy for him and Rebecca to find a way for them to live in relative peace. But this seemed to be the wrong path to that end.

The hospital was busy as usual, and the hall to Bartholomew's intensive care room was crowded with police and other hangers on. Peter tried to evade the emerging figure of someone from the newspaper The Sun. If these people got wind of things it would be very bad for the Team indeed.

Fortunately, he saw Rebecca's fair head among those who were milling about outside the Bartholomew hospital room. Peter went around and strove to catch Rebecca's eye. She looked forlorn, almost lost, and it made him feel awful.

She saw him finally. He made a motion to meet somewhere. She nodded her head and then went out of sight.

Peter was in the more private area where the doctors and the family met. It was deserted. She went to him and they embraced. "I'm very sorry, my love." He said in her ear.

She started to cry. "No, don't. It's alright. He should pull through." Peter gritted his jaw at this blatant lie.

"No, Peter." Rebecca said through tears. "I'm afraid they said he's not going to make it. He's in the surgery. It might be any time soon. It's terrible. How could this happen? He's a surgeon, for heaven's sake. A damn good one."

He didn't say anything to that.

"I suppose you don't know what else one can do?" She looked up at him expectantly.

"No. I am not any expert in these medical matters. Your mother, is she alright?"

"That's the other thing. She's so totally messed up. I'm afraid she's not going to be well for a while. They were so close. He loved her and she loved him. I can't tell what more to do - do I go back home with her and help her get her life together? Look," she shook her head, "I'm talking like he's dead now."

Peter tried to hug her more tightly but she felt as though her words had now got in between them. "I'll help, I will. You need to trust things will be taken care of."

"I have to see if I need to take a long vacation. I am not sure I'm up for one. I've only started working there."

"Let's wait for the surgeon to tell us."

Rebecca lifted her tearstained face to his. "I don't want to leave, Peter. I really don't want to leave. Mom was good, but now that Dad might be gone she'll have to rely on me. There isn't anyone else. Well, maybe there is. But the grandparents - they aren't any good. Too full of their own problems." Rebecca wiped her tears away.

"Why don't we sit and wait." Peter said with a sigh. It wasn't his expertise to comfort people. It wasn't taught at the MI5 briefing rooms.

They sat in silence, and while they did, they held hands. Peter studied Rebecca's face. He saw that her face had become more robust, as though - damn, he thought, he forgot she was pregnant. It made him more and more frantic. It was almost as though the words were written on the wall. He was going to have to handle this pregnancy of hers. How it would be handled was something he had to grapple with as well

"I'm hoping we can go find a place to eat - are you on for dinner tonight?" He asked, making it sound light.

"I think so. If Mom's ok, can she come along?"

"I'd like to see you alone. She will be alright for a few hours I'm sure."

"I am not that sure. She's not ever been so blindsided as this. Mom's really like a Southern girl, very delicate and very much the type to need taking care of."

"No, I don't think she's like that. I think she'll be fine. I'll see if they can find someone who can come and take her home. I'll see if that can be handled like that."

Rebecca looked puzzled. "You want her to go back alone?"

"We have some unfinished business, you and I."

"We do." She sounded unconvinced. Then, the dawning of what she and he had made gave her face a different glow. "Oh Peter."

"Yes, Oh Peter indeed." He laughed at her. "Now, let's try not to worry about things. Your Dad will probably not make it. I don't want you to get into a state of mind that will endanger things."

"How?" She asked him the unfinished question.

"I know."

They laughed and then she hugged him tightly. "Oh my dear Peter!"

"Don't be sad then ok? I'll be with you all the time. You and I."

A knock came to the door. They looked up. A man in his early thirties entered. He looked at Rebecca with a concerned look. "Hi, darling Rebecca."

"Oh, Cor!" Rebecca said, with consternation.

"I heard the bad news. Are you alright?" He strode into the room, ignored Peter and took Rebecca's hand in his.

She removed her hand and kept close to Peter. "This is my - er- ex. Corcoran."

"Ralph. Corcoran." The man nodded at Peter

who looked at him with a stone faced expression,
"Rebecca and I are having a temporary problem with our
engagement."

"Is that so?" Peter said smoothly. "Rebecca and
I have just got engaged ourselves. We don't think you
should stay."

Corcoran stepped back. "Is that true, Rebecca?"

"Yes. It's true."

He slunk into himself. "I'm dashed upset.
Surprised. I never knew. I can't believe it."

"Believe it and then leave us." Peter said gruffly.

"Ok, ok. I'm leaving. I wanted to see if I could
be of any service. Is your mother anywhere?"

"She's - "

"I think you'd better leave Corcoran." Peter said
with growing irritation.

Corcoran left them and closed the door behind

him.

"If that man ever bothers you again tell me." Peter said evenly. "I'm fed up with that overgrown schoolboy."

Rebecca was silent. "I've not been very successful with getting him to realize I'm not any longer his fiancee."

"Were you ever serious? Or was this a fling?"

"I wasn't myself. I was eager to find something more than living in the place where I've been for most of my life. Everyone was beginning to look the same, want the same things, wanting to get ahead and I was tired of being the boss' daughter and I felt as though those who hated him were making my life miserable. He was a good surgeon, but he made people feel bad for helping him save lives."

"Oh, that kind of medico."

"Yes. He thought it would make them toe the line if he was displeased or if they didn't work with him the right way. He lost a few good people because of it. And, we were wealthy, Mom didn't have to work at all, and she was in with the society groups. She was and is a very fragile woman."

"How did you ever get the gumption to live in this place, hundreds of miles away from home?"

"Well, I suppose I used Cor. I was - well, I wasn't a good girl that way. I wish we didn't discuss this. I'm not proud of my life when I was at Connecticut. It isn't a life I want for anyone of my close friends or, my - er - baby."

"Yes." He said no more. Peter leaned back and closed his eyes.

She was silent as well. "I'm sorry Peter. I'm thinking you aren't as excited as you were to say you loved me."

"I am too. I seem to feel as though I've gotten what I deserve."

Rebecca started to cry and with a great deal of remorse and feeling. He tried to give her a hug but she turned away.

Peter stood up and tried to figure out what had to be done. "Look, why don't you dry your tears. Let's get some dinner in an hour. I'll try to talk to some people about arranging for your fathers remains to return to Connecticut. Then your mother will have to discuss things with the psychiatrist on duty. Is she on any medications for nerves?"

"No, I don't believe so."

"Good. At least she will be taken care of. If you want her to stay till the end of their vacation here, that will be fine. But she will have to return to Connecticut.

How old is she?"

"She's 54."

"And your relatives - do they live close to your house in Connecticut?"

"They are - her brother Richard, Richard Kelly, lives near us. I -"

"I'll call him. Just give me his contact information. Then we'll think of what you need to do."

She said nothing but brushed another tear away. Peter began to feel so very uneasy with his own feelings that it made it so clear to them both that they were skirting what might be the very issue they ought to talk about

The door opened again and this time the surgeon came through the door. He was looking unhappy and his surgical gown was smeared with blood. "Hi, I'm Mr. Crane. I just worked on your father, Miss

Bartholomew."

"What's the verdict?" Demanded Peter.

"I'm sorry. He's gone."

Rebecca sighed and then she sat down after rising with Peter.

"I see." She said.

"I'll talk to your mother now."

"Make sure she's got a psychiatrist in the room with her."

"Of course." The surgeon looked at Peter with some concern. Then he left.

Peter turned to Rebecca and took her hand. "I want you and me to have a quiet dinner tonight. We'll get something on the way home. I'll make sure a guard will be at your door tonight. Then, tomorrow you'll have to tell your office about going on funeral leave. Ok?"

"Ok," Rebecca replied wanly.

Chapter Twenty-Eight

Margo was typing furiously in her laptop as she followed along with the conversation that she was listening to in her digital recorder. The opening of the door did not register and only when the sigh of Moorhead across from her as he sat down heavily made her stop. She looked at him. Then she turned off the recorder and sat back, her arms across her chest. "You look like the devil." She said coolly. "Too hot out there today, eh?"

"Like beastly. Watkins and Peter, and then this cad Bartholomew getting shiv'd, then Perkins. It's way too hot to handle. I'm not happy that I'm in this sort of mission. It's all going to hell, Margo dear. I'd advise you to take a long trip out of here, somewhere there's no cell phones, no people who know you, and lots and lots of drinks with umbrellas on them." Moorhead grinned briefly then his face returned to being morose.

'I see." She looked sad and turned off her laptop folding it with a snap.

"No, I'm sad about Peter. He's not going to be very happy forever. I'm thinking he happened on this tail I did and now he seems to have to this Bartholomew daughter pregnant and now he's really in the soup - she is and he is well - shall we say they're in love but perhaps he's feeling caught in a bind."

"What about the guy Bartholomew. Was he

passing something indeed?"

"The information never got to us, if he were one of our group. No, it's with Perkins' men. Which causes us a great deal of anxiety. Perkins' got his own band of people and nobody knows who they are. But, we know there's a man and we've got a slightly blurred picture of the package."

"I think that before Bartholomew arrived here he was in conference in a New York meeting. He loves being in all these International meets, and that is how these medicos get involved with the whole espionage thing."

"Margo you good girl. How great you think that." Moorhead reached over and mussed her already untidy head. "Now, if we only got a few more tidbits, we can find out who gave him what."

"That would be good. I took it upon myself to

talk to some of the Perkins people, pretending to be their best friend."

"Really?" Moorhead was transfixed.

"Yes, we are like this, Perkins and myself - or at least, his people are." She held two fingers up twisted together.

"Do tell."

"For starters, Perkins has a predilection for women of a certain style. The fair and buxom ones. Very predictable, aren't these men? And, therefore he's got so much dirt on him we know he's got to be the very one who'll lead us to Revenor."

Moorhead looked more interested. "I am so very envious. You women. I can't believe how you can be so very very —"

"At a loss for words?"

"I am."

"I think my hunch is that Perkins and Revenor have a person in between them."

"Elena Ramos?"

"Not exactly." Margo went to a file cabinet and pulled out a photograph. She handed it to Moorhead.

"Who's this dishy girl?"

"She happens to be one of Revenor's friends. Grew up with some chums from Oxford. She's a psychiatrist. Name of Lucinda Chillingworth. She has been trying to lure some of her more attractive patients to be friends with Revenor."

"Oh. Ah."

"I think if we got to that stupid weekend thing they're trying to court everyone with gonads to, we might be able to name names and see things that only God can."

"Margo, you are the soul of information."

Moorhead laughed softly.

Chapter Twenty-Nine

Later that evening, Peter and Rebecca ate in her apartment. They spoke to each other normally, as though they had done all this before, getting the food warmed up from the take away and setting the table, and then getting the wine out of the fridge and putting down napkins. Peter observed Rebecca as she went from one place in the kitchen to the dining table and back. She wasn't her usual cheerful self, which was to be expected.

He decided to hang back and let her get her own thoughts together before they would speak more intimately. The idea of being with her hung in their thoughts and it was making both of them a bit scared. It seemed to Peter that their relationship had begun in the middle and now they were tasked to make the beginning and then tie it all to the proper ending - a proper conclusion and have the strings tied up in a neat bow.

#

She asked, "Do you wish to have some dessert? I took time to make a custard pie."

"Custard pie?" He sounded unsure.

"You've had this before, haven't you? I have had it for years. Favorite thing."

"Well, then I'll have some."

"Ok, fine." She went to the fridge again and took out the pie. She took a long time unwrapping it and

Peter had to crane his neck to see what she was up to.

"Do you need help?"

"NO." She sounded upset now.

"What's wrong?"

"Oh."

"Oh what?"

"Just don't say anything. I've had a bad day altogether."

"Oh alright, fine. I'm not that hungry."

She looked disappointed. "You're not that hungry?"

"I mean I could get hungry but if you're not into eating that would be fine with me,"

"I am not hungry either."

"Let's eat anyway."

She brought the pie to the table and then sat down. They looked at the food and then Peter picked up his fork and started to eat. They were silent as they ate and in between, Peter would make a noise as though he was enjoying the food. "Did you cook this?"

"Yes." Rebecca's face became more crumpled with emotion.

He looked up and said, "Hey what's the matter?"

"I don't know." She started to cry.

He took her hand and took her to the living room. "I'm not sure why you're crying."

"I don't know why."

"Tell me why."

"I don't think you love me." She said, finally letting go of gusts of sobbing.

He pulled her close and let her heave against him. "Dear Rebecca, I love you. I wasn't sure until that awful cad Corcoran came in to intrude. But I do love you. Don't cry now. Is that all that you're upset about?"

"No. I'm very frightened. I lost my Dad today and my Mom's not able to function right. I'm scared I have to go and take care of her forever. And we'd never see each other again." She went into another gale of weeping. It made him even more sad to think of her words.

"No, you and I will be together soon and permanently. I will take care of everything. Your Mom will see a psychiatrist and I'll pay for it. And then she'll be right as rain and you will be telling her soon that we will be married. Ok?"

"Oh. Ok."

"Are you sure you're ok?"

"Yes." She became more relaxed and then she turned her face against his shoulder and let him hold her.

Peter looked up and wondered whether this was going to work. His career was over, surely, he thought.

And that meant he had to let go of whatever operation was going on with Watkins' and Moorhead's work. He also had to tell Elena that he wasn't interested in her any longer. The list of things he was to do made him somewhat limp with exhaustion.

But he was holding a woman who had gotten under his skin, and given him the worst blindside in his life. It seemed unreal but here was how they were and it seemed as though it would work. If only God had any hand in it, he thought determinedly.

Rebecca stirred in his arms and moved a little away. "There's more."

"Oh?" Peter gave her a look, as though he didn't want to hear anymore.

"I'm pregnant."

"Really?"

"I've not seen the doctor or anything, but I am

pretty sure I'm pregnant."

"Are you sure it's mine?"

"Yes, damn it, it's your baby." Rebecca almost fell of her chair as she tried to get away from him. "I'm sorry Peter. I know it's a sudden thing but I did do that gadget thing. It said 'positive'".

"I see."

She waited a bit and then looked at him. "I guess we weren't exactly wearing protection."

"And you're not on any contraceptive."

"No. I've not been since I left Cor."

"Why is that?"

"I don't know - I felt sick when I was on it. Had a bad feeling whenever it was time for my period to happen,"

"Oh."

"So there. I'm pregnant. I will see the doctor

sometime. I have all this to think of. I suppose that changes everything. You don't have to do anything, Peter. I will have the baby."

"So you aren't going to get rid of it?"

"NO!!!"

"Oh I didn't realize you were very adamant about it. That's good. For you."

"For me?"

"Well, I am glad you're not the type of girl who'll get rid of an unwanted child." He sat, lounging and yet every fiber of his being was on the alert.

"Unwanted child." Rebecca repeated slowly. "I want this child, Peter. I know we've only known each other a short time. I will have this child. You don't need to worry."

He stood up and paced the floor and then stopped. "You don't want me to be involved in raising this child, is that what you're saying?"

"I don't know what you would want. I think you might be thinking I got you into this predicament. Even though you made love to me and initiated it all."

He put a hand and raked his hair. "I'm very glad you're pregnant. It's just that it puts a bit of a awkward spin into my life."

"Well, you don't have to marry me if you don't want to. Babies like ours are somehow an unwanted consequence of a great sex life. Or a one night stand."

"I guess I'm to blame yes, for everything, I saw you that night you looked beautiful in that dress, and then you were so appealing and it all made me go nuts. I had to have you and I did and we had a lovely lovely time, and now…"

"We did and I loved it all of it, and I want to keep us together but not with the baby as the sort of tie that I envisioned us to have together. I didn't realize I was - I did not think of taking any contraception at all when I thought I might become someone in your life."

"When did you think I would be someone in your life?" Peter's brow lifted with interest.

She looked flustered. "I don't know - maybe when you asked me to dinner. And then before that when you came looking for Elena. And then before that when we met at the coffee book place."

"Yes, I think that might have crossed my mind too."

"Well, so we were thinking like that separately and then we got into an affair."

Peter sat down again. "Look, I'm ready to help in any way. You know that I still love you but this is definitely something that I now have to think a great deal about. My job, Rebecca, is not your ordinary nine to five job in the City. I'm a man who works for the government."

"Go on."

"You want me to tell you point blank."

"You're beginning to scare me."

"I'm someone who's working with MI5, have you heard of it?"

She looked at him with a frown. "I have."

"You seem to be unhappy about this revelation."

"I am aware of the MI5 but I now think it is going to be very hard for us to be together, is that what you're saying?"

It was Peter's cue to either say yes or not exactly. His mind wavered and he looked at her face and then he looked at her belly, which seemed still to be relatively the same size as when he last saw her. "I quit them the other day. I told them I was in love with you. Now I'm going to have to tell you that we need to be still on the outs. It's very important now to pretend we aren't together. The thing that happened to your father - his murder - it has something to do with what I used to do."

"Oh my God." Rebecca's face was ashen. "He - You - ?"

"I'm not sure how he had got into this but it's - I mean there's evidence that he's been dishonest. Not in the way you think but, well, there's evidence."

"He's a good man, Peter. I never knew him to be dishonest in his job. Everyone held him in awe at home. He did a good job and saved many people's lives. His surgical skills were so far above anyone else's. But now you say there's evidence he's dishonest?"

"Many people in life look as though they are the God's honest people that ever walked the earth. But they aren't and they won't ever be. They just know how to show to people the side that they think will give them a pass, or make them acceptable in life to the important groups they wish to infiltrate. Do you understand?"

Rebecca nodded slowly. "Then I'm sunk. I don't know how to go about life now. I am beginning to suspect everyone."

"I should think that way. But that is me. That's how I operate. I should now have got you to a point where I need to silence you -"

She looked at him, aghast. "Silence me?" Then it dawned on her. "Yes, you will need to. I'm very sad that - it sounds like a hokey old spy story, but it is true, you need to do that, don't you?"

There was a pause and he felt very much like he'd stepped all over her life by being her lover.

"I'm very sorry. I'm telling you this because I don't think our life together, if we wanted to raise this

baby together, will be good. I'm so deep into this MI5
that even if I'm out of there I'll still be somehow
connected, and those who are out for my blood will be
waiting somewhere, and you, you my innocent girl, will
be somewhere shopping at the local Tesco and the little
baby cooing at the basket in front of you, and then
suddenly, that scene will be all black and then I'll be
looking for you and the baby everywhere and then I will
realize that this little family of mine will not ever have a
good ending."

Rebecca swallowed hard. "It's my luck to have
fallen for you, Peter. I really feel defeated, so very sad,
so very sad…".

They spoke little after that. There were no
solutions given. No suggestions.

Peter said after a long pause, "Look, I'm going to
pretend that I knew you from the usual connections.

Elena and I are engaged, and you were a friend of hers and I happened to hear about what happened to you because we did have a short affair, and now, I'm forced to help you with whatever you need. You will have to return to the USA and take your Mother along. Then I will go back to my life and try to see what I can do to disengage myself from what I've done for over twenty years."

"Ok. That sounds like a plan."

"You don't mind."

"No. I feel like I've gone through the ringer with our affair. You were too good to be true, weren't you? You were the one that I felt strongly about. Now," She looked at something beside her. The tears began to fall again but she made no sound. "I think I'll have to go see Mom now and -"

"No. She's fine and it's not good to go out in

this late hour."

"Fine. Then if you will excuse me, I will need to go to bed."

"I can't let you go to bed. You need to stay up for a while and then I will go but I will ask a police man to stand next to your front door. Is that ok?"

"Yes." She stood up and wiped a tear from her face. Even that movement made Peter wish he could take her into his arms. But so many words have been said and they were now at an awkward state between them.

"Good. I'll send for an officer and then you will need to do whatever you wish to do. I'll sit in the living room and you don't have to do anything else with me."

Rebecca left and went to do something in the sink. Her face was stony and yet her emotions were churning inside her chest. She felt no real movement inside her, as though the baby would move, but it was all she could do to keep from hating everything that she had ever gone through. This was the place, London, where she would go and strike anew, and live a life apart from Cor, and make a life for herself. But now, her father was dead and his reputation was in shreds. Her mother was on sedatives and sleeping the sleep that offered no solace at all. It was grim to her that the love she felt for Peter had now become as business like as he said at the last time he spoke. She took up a knife that lay on the sink and stared at it. The pull of this knife made her swoon and then she hastily washed it and put it away.

By the end of the washing up, she was truly feeling her emotions get the best of her. She hadn't even thought of her father with all this conversation with Peter about them and the baby. Now she had to mourn three things - her affairs was gone, her father whom she loved was dead, and her mother, the only other person in her life (save the baby inside her) was facing life without her own love.

Later, she changed into her nightclothes and put on a flannel gown over it. She did not go out and stayed instead in her room. It made her feel like a lost child and she hated the idea that she now wasn't free to go out and do whatever popped into her head. The last image she had of what Peter described was now haunting her. If they did have this baby, and the baby and her were out and doing things - God, how was that going to be? Would she be safe all the way in Connecticut? Would it be anywhere that she could be safe, even though nobody would know it was Peter's child?

There was a knock on her bedroom door. "It's Peter. The officer's now on standby at your door."

"Thank you, Peter."

"If there's nothing else, I'm going to take off. I will try to contact you sometime."

"Ok."

"I'm going to give you an obstetrician's name. She will be safe. I wouldn't talk about the baby to anyone, ok?"

"Yes, ok."

After a silence, she heard nothing of his departure and she pulled her blanket up to her chin. Her eyes looked up staring at the ceiling and then after a while, she fell asleep.

Chapter Thirty

The first sound in the morning that came to Rebecca's
ears was that of her cell phone ringing outside in the
kitchen. She tossed the covers off her, and got out, her
mind awhirl. She'd slept a few hours then she awoke
and got scared all over again then she decided it was a
waste of time to sleep any longer. She didn't seem to
feel any biliousness from her pregnancy. That had
occurred since she saw her Mother and today that

seemed not be happening.

She fairly ran to the kitchen and picked up the cell phone. "Hello?" Her voice was breathless.

"It's Mom - how are you?" Her mother sounded strained, solemn, unrecognizable. It sounded as though Sophia had been crying and her voice was raw.

"I'm ok."

"I"m fucking not. I am not happy at all. I am not happy Rebecca, I'm so fucking mad and I don't know why. It's just that your father is dead and nobody is telling me why." The sobs came and then both were crying,

"Oh my God, Mom."

"I am so fucking mad. I am either mad or so very sad and grief stricken. I am so fucking all over the hell with being mad and I want to end this nightmare. I want to see Leo again, looking like he would in his clothes and his smile and all of that. Now I can't I have

got a phone call to see to his remains and all that crap. I

am so upset and I wish we never came here, Rebecca,

You and I need to talk about this."

"Mom - "

"No, you won't make me stop this feeling it is

something I need to feel. Otherwise I'll fall apart and

you will have a mother who's going to be so out of it

with all sorts of pills -"

"Ok Mom, I'll come over. I'll see about taking

you a few things to eat."

"No, don't take any food. We will meet at the

hotel restaurant and then we will talk about how to go

about this next day or two - or week. How you and I

need to find some kind of - hell, what do we find about

this stuff?"

Rebecca had never heard her mother speak in

such profane language before so she realized that her mother had become so very incensed and she was fighting mad. At whom, she guessed it was the Government, or it seemed it was. Rebecca stood on her heels and listened to more of her mother raging.

"I"m going to talk to some people, and the embassy will know about this, and I'll even guess I could discuss this with the news from the USA. What do you think, Rebecca? This kind of thing should NEVER happen to anyone who's visiting this lousy country."

"Mom you need to calm down."

"I'm only warming up, Rebecca."

"Well I don't want you to get so out of whack that you'll knock somebody down when you see them on the way to the restaurant."

"No, dear daughter." Her mother's voice became sweet. "I''ll be so damn polite it will make them so very uncomfortable. I'm sure I can talk to the Chief of Scotland Yard if I had to. I am a wealthy American woman, aren't I? And with that comes a great deal of what ever it is that Americans are good at. Mainly, causing a big stir. That's what I think!"

Rebecca hid a smile and then decided to go along with her mother. "Ok, Mom. I'll change and we'll have breakfast. Ok?"

"Fine." Her mother hung up with a click.

The morning went fast for Rebecca, as she got out of her nightwear and into a serviceable pants outfit. She looked out at the window and saw that it had begun to snow. She pulled on a pair of good boots that would keep her from slipping in the snow and then took her light overcoat with her. She forgot to pick up her bag so she had to go back and find it.

When she got out of there apartment, she surprised the officer and he touched his hat as he saw her. "G'morning Miss. I'm guessing you're on your way out?" He looked at her nervously.

"Yes. I need to go see my Mother."

"Fine. I'll er - I'll go with you. That is if you think so. I've not been given orders to follow you. Can you possibly hang on while I call HQ?"

She paused. "Ok."

He turned around and got on his phone.

"Yes, she's going off to see her Mum. Is that ok? You need me to go with her? Ok, fine. Thank you."

He faced her and said, "I'll need to escort you there. Someone else will accompany you when you decide to - um- go somewhere else. You are still planning to go to work?"

She realized it was a weekday. "Oh, heck. Yes, I
need to. But I'll call them and tell them what
happened."

"Oh alright then. Shall we? I've not got a car
with me. You plan to get a taxi, or are you - well, now,
how do I do this? I think we need a - "

"Taxi, yes." She finished for him. If she made
it to her mother's hotel, then she would have
accomplished something big.

Her mother was as beautiful as ever, wearing a dark gray
suit and looking as though not a hard was out of place in
her head. Sophia was already having coffee and the
waiter was placing another cup for Rebecca.

"Hi Mom."

"There you are." Sophia's demeanor was so very

different. It seemed as though her years being a wealthy, gracious hostess to her husband's many different luncheons, dinners and balls had become congealed into this woman who could do anything. Rebecca suspected that the sedative was active in her Mom's behavior today. "I'm glad you're here. Sit and let's talk."

"Can we at least have something to eat?" Rebecca sat down. The waiter lingered at her words. "I'll have a French toast, eggs over easy - two, and some ham please."

He nodded and left.

"Now," Sophia said coolly. "I've not spoken to anyone in the States yet. I did talk to your uncle Dick. He said he will arrange for Leo - I mean your father's - body to get transferred to the USA. It will mean a TON of money, Rebecca. I am sick of that idea. Now, I also want to tell you that you won't talk about it to your friends at work. I won't make a scandal unless someone fucks up and makes me even more irate."

"Yes, Mom."

"I have until the end of the week to get things squared away. So - "

"I'm fine with whatever you wish to do."

They sat in silence for a while. It seemed as though the pent up emotions had become diluted in the quiet atmosphere of the restaurant. The snow outside had become worse, and globs of white powdery snow fell to the ground. The people who walked on the ground outside became unable to navigate well as the snow diminished visibility.

The food came and Rebecca ate with relish. She was not too happy but it was a way to relieve her sadness - to dig into food that would nourish her and give her strength. It didn't taste that good to her but she gave it a good dose of salt and pepper and some spicy flakes of pepper that the restaurant thought would be a good addition to the table.

"I'm sure you want to go home soon Mom."

"Ah - we need to know what you are planning to do now, Rebecca."

"I'm not sure - what's going to happen. Is Dad's body going home and there will be the funeral et cetera?"

"Of course!" Sophia sounded affronted. "I'm not burying him here."

"Oh, I wasn't thinking that. I was kind of well - I don't now what to do. Do you - Do I - go with you and then help with the funeral and then - ah - do I come back here? And work as usual? What will happen to you, Mom?"

Sophia looked sad. "I think you need to find out

what you want your life to be and if it's still to live here, after all that's happened, then go on with it. I'll be fine. I have a lot of friends and well, I'll be alone. I mean, I don't think I'll meet anyone like your father again." Sophia tried not to give into the emotion her words called up in her mind.

"I might not stay here after all, Mom."

"If that's what you think then fine. You and I will go back to our home and you'll be alright. You've got your friends don't you? Have you even got in contact with them?"

"No."

"Well you should keep in touch with them. They will be so very shocked at the news."

Rebecca felt as though the tension in her body was making her hurt everywhere. "I - ah - told Peter about the baby."

Sophia uttered a soft oath. "Oh, my dear Rebecca. On top of everything else."

"I am really sad to tell you that Peter and I aren't going to do anything for this baby. I'll raise it if it does get born, and make a home for it wherever it might be."

"Good. Damn that man. How dare he get you pregnant. I don't know about these English anymore. Did I tell you that your father and I were thinking of us retiring here so we could be closer together? I hate that we thought this was the place to stay to live life to its end."

"I guess it's not." Rebecca sipped her coffee. She reached for the coffee pot and poured herself another cup, mixed sugar and cream in it and then sipped it once again. "I'm thinking this was a one night stand. It sounded like he thought it too. I guess things were misunderstood."

"You fell in love with him."

"Yes, I did. He wasn't like Cor. Cor was charming and made me feel as though life was a game, and that got me to realize he was a drug addict, and a gambler and a woman kept him so he could go and buy drugs and gamble all over again,"

"Rebecca!" Sophia looked at her with shock.

"Yeah. He wasn't the one. He wants me back but I won't go back to that life. It was hell and I am sad I fell for the facade."

"I know. The English tend to make you think they're the bees knees." Sophia nodded and stabbed at her potato dish.

"Well, I'm ready to turn in my badge and resign at work, but I need to take some time to think about what I'll do." Rebecca said leaning back and trying to feel as though this would be a normal thing with her. "It's funny, Mom, how things worked the way they did."

"You fell in love with London. I can see why. You fell in love with an Englishman. Twice. Then well, it's like that story where the coach becomes squash and the mice and all that sort of fairy tale they tell you really happened."

After a pause, Rebecca said, "I'm going to have to get myself seen by the OB."

"Good. I'll let you go now. I have to call Dick again and see what other things are needed to get Leo back home. I also need to call the bank and find out about paying the airlines and then I'll see if I can - you can fly back on your own after you've decided what to do. Don't rush to go to the funeral. I'm feeling so lost myself."

"I feel the same way. I can't handle traveling now that I'm pregnant."

The officer came to their table. "Miss, Mr. Reed wanted me to give you this." He handed her a card.

"Thanks," said Rebecca.

"Who's that?" Sophia asked, curious.

"Oh, he's the police officer who stood by my apartment last night to keep me from getting in trouble."

"Why? What trouble is that?"

"Well, uh, in case the guy who killed Dad tried to come after me."

"That's funny. I never got a police escort. I'm feeling bothered by the idea that your Dad's murderer might be after you or me!"

"I don't think that Peter thought that. He just wanted to make sure I was ok."

"Well, I still never got police protection." Sophia gave a sigh that belied her anger. "I'm sick of this. Who is this Peter you know? How does he know these cops

and why does he get a cop to stand by your apartment
door?"

Rebecca stared back at her mother. "He's a
solicitor's assistant."

"He is a solicitor's assistant?"

"Yes, he's used to working with the police, I
guess."

"Well, that was real nice of him to give YOU
protection." Sophia looked upset. "I am ready to leave
this town, Rebecca. Oh!"

Rebecca looked guiltily at her mother.

Sophia was rifled through her purse and took out
a credit card to pay the bill. "Here, dear, why don't you
go off and get to work. I see it's a lot of snow out there.
Get a cab. Oh I'll need to regroup later with you. Or we
can just call each other. I'm so very confused, upset and
still mad as a hornet. I think I'll have to find that shrink

they gave me to talk to. What was his name?"

Rebecca stood and then as an afterthought, kissed her mother's dark head before heading out the lobby.

She went out the entrance, became buffeted by gobs of snowflakes, large as ever like softballs impinging on her figure. There were no taxis to be had and that meant she needed to find another means of transportation. A cough sounded beside her and Rebecca turned to see the police officer next to her. "You need to get back to your place, Miss?"

"Oh! I forgot you were there. I need to get to my office."

"I'd be careful Miss. You stand by and I'll get a cab for you." He disappeared into the lobby briefly. He returned and as he came to her side, a taxi slid into view in front of them.

"Thank you!" She said with a smile.

"No problem, Miss."

Chapter Thirty-One

The City of London was enveloped in a deep fog the morning after Leo was murdered. Inside the labyrinths of London's streets, right around the church of St. Paul's, was a grey building. There were no signs on the front but it seemed as though it was a common office building that housed varied and sundry businesses. People came in through the revolving doors and left through the same. A man in a leather jacket stopped briefly in front of the building and consulted his cell phone. He had a briefcase in his hand, and looked swarthy, but had a military bearing.

He took himself into the reception area where only a woman clad in a drab brown suit with a necklace that bore a picture ID greeted him wanly. "Hi," said the man in the leather jacket. His accent was not English but it might have passed for a Yorkshire accent. "Looking for the Humboldt Publishing Company. Is it anywhere upstairs?"

The woman looked at him with boredom in her eyes then consulted a rolodex in front of her. She looked into one of the leaves of the rolodex. The man decided she was stupid, or, new at her job. "It's on the fifth floor, room number 745."

"Thanks," he said briefly and moved towards the bank of elevators behind her.

The elevator ride was a bit choppy, and he decided it was an old building, and he smiled slightly as if in approval.

He got off, checked which way Room 745 was located by the signage, and walked briskly to his right. The sign of Humboldt Publishing came into view, hanging securely against a broad door that had a glass part where he could see the people inside. He saw several people passing by his line of view. Emboldened, he entered the office without knocking.

The office area was large, and peopled with serious looking office workers. It was his decision to find somebody to talk to. But he was accosted by a man who looked at him with some suspicion. "Need help?" He demanded of the man in the leather jacket.

"I'm looking for Mr Jack Perkins. I'm here to deliver a package."

"Oh," the man paused, then in his mind, made up a decision to respond. "Follow me. Who did you say you were?"

"Oh, yeah, I'm George Clearadge. From the printer's."

"What's the name of the printer?"

"Lorrimer's Printing. Down by the docks. It's been there for ages. Heard of it, I'm sure."

The man ignored his additional information and led him down a narrow hallway where they met with more office personnel. Several looked at George and then looked again when they saw who was escorting him inside the office inner sanctum.

The door where they stopped at was half open. Inside was a man in shirtsleeves and suspenders standing with the phone in his ear. The man was barking into the phone a few terse orders before he hung up. George drew back as if scared, and then he was in the presence

of this man, who said he was Jack Perkins.

"Mr George Clearadge. From - ah - Lorrimer's

Printing."

"I've come to deliver the editor's copy, Mr.

Perkins." George said mildly.

"Hand it over." The man was an American.

There was a frown between his bushy eyebrows.

George gave him the thick envelope.

"Thanks."

"You're welcome."

"Are you a courier of some sort or did you come

from the printer's?"

"I - we don't have couriers, sir. Just people to

deliver. If that's all, I'll leave now."

Perkins took hold of the envelope and then

ordered his man and George to leave him.

George went off with the man who got him to Perkins' office and sighed with relief. "God, that wasn't a nice man, was it?"

"I'll not say." Replied his escort before disappearing into an office, leaving George to find his way out.

Perkins took his time to examine the outside of the envelope. It was addressed to him but to the wrong address. It made him pause but he decided it was part of the subterfuge. Damn subterfuge. He thought. It was getting too warm for him in London, he mused to himself. He looked at the seal and decided it had not been tampered with. Then he took the penknife and slashed the envelope's flap open. Before he could say a word, a few powdery bits came flying out into his face.

The white powder flew out and flew out, and then Perkins became distinctly aware that this was all a fatal event and he was in a tearing hurry to leave his office. But he couldn't leave because his legs became leaden, and he fell over on his way out of his desk.

George Clearadge was about a block and a half away from the building he met Perkins at and decided it was all too foggy to walk so he hailed a cab and told the cab driver where he wanted to go. As they pulled away from the curb, an emergency vehicle with its lights flashing and siren wailing passed them by and slid into a stop by the same grey building that George was in a few minutes ago. George looked at the vehicle and then sat back, his face imperturbable. "Well, that didn't take long."

Chapter Thirty-Two

The cab drove past a Baker's street pub and divulged George from its interior. "Thanks, man." George said with a wave, after giving the cab driver his tip.

He walked into the bar and slid into one of the dark mahogany booths. A waitress came by, her glossy hair swinging and her hand holding a notepad. "Hey, I'm here to get something to eat - can you give me a menu?"

"Sure thing." The woman left and passed the red headed customer who was hunkered over his full English. She leaned over next to the red headed man and asked the barkeep for a menu. "Need a menu. Chap's not familiar with the fare."

"Here you are love." The barkeep handed her the menu and then went off to shove an aluminum handled ice scoop into the bucket of ice.

"I'm sure it's going to be a horrible day." Said someone in the rear of the pub.

"Foggy as all get out."

"Can't stand it. Can't see a thing. I'm sure everyone is here because it's so damn foggy."

"Yeah."

The redheaded man looked up. "That's why I'm here." He grinned cheerily.

The waitress went to George and smiled. "Here's

the menu, love. Take your time."

"I certainly will." He grabbed the menu and pored over the list of breakfast items.

The television in the corner squawked and a news man declared the weather was going to be foggy for another day. Everyone groaned at this.

The waitress came back. "Have you decided?"

"I'll have some bangers and mash. And a pot of coffee."

"That is all?"

"Oh and maybe some sauerkraut for the bangers, if you have them," he added without much ado.

"Uh." She stood, fanning herself mindlessly. "We don't make sauerkraut."

"Oh that's too bad." George frowned. "I had a hankering for some sauerkraut."

"We have some picalilly."

"Picalilly?" He repeated. Then a smile spread on his face. "Ah, that'll do. I don't mind the mustard. But it will do. Thanks." Then he grabbed her hand before she could leave. "I'll have the pot of coffee now, if you please."

She looked down at his hand on hers and gave him a look of askance. "You will, if you let my hand free, you toad."

The redheaded man disappeared from the bar. The waitress went to the kitchen and tossed off her apron. "Here, this is what that horrible ass that came in wants. I'm needing to go to the loo, ok?" She handed the order to the chef and left the kitchen.

She made her way to the part where the loo was located but instead of going in, she kept going into the back and then opened a door. There, the redheaded man sat with his eyes on the television. "That is way too much. I am sure that is way too much. Did he even want to handle me? I ask you, Moorhead." Margo complained and sat down with a flourish. She swung her dark hair and then she leaned forward.

"Mmm." Moorhead said.

They looked at each other. Then he held up a hand and she held up hers and they had a five which was their code that something went well.

The office of Watkins *et al.* was seemingly empty. The telephone rang and rang. The lights were on but nobody seemed to be around. Finally, there was a click where the telephone was directed to the voice mail.

Silence reigned. After some time, the door to Mr Watkin's office opened and he stepped out with a folder in his hand. "Michelle, are you there?"

She was not anywhere to be found. Watkins walked around to the other office where he would stay when someone was visiting. It was empty. He heard the phone ring once again and with a shrug, he went to pick it up. Mr Watkins was not averse to answering his own telephone. "Hello?"

"Hello, is it possible to speak with Mr. Watkins? It's a matter of importance."

"This is Watkins. Who are you?"

"This is the office of Mr Jack Perkins."

"Yes?"

"You know him I understand. "

"If I do it isn't a close association. Why are you

calling?"

"Mr Perkins asked us to call you in case he was called in ill."

"Yes, I see. Well, is he ill?"

"Yes, in fact, he's dead."

"Is that a fact? How he die?" Watkins leaned back with an interested expression in his face. As he did so, Peter Reed entered the room and motioned he would see him in Watkin's office.

"He had a - a - "

"Spill it out, man."

"Someone came to deliver a package and it contained some anthrax like material, but we believe he was gassed by a very sophisticated type of vehicle that carried the toxin straight into his lungs. He died almost immediately."

"When did this happen?"

"A couple of hours ago. His body is in the morgue but it's really quite a bad scene. All personnel have been evacuated and there's been a great deal of hue and cry. Terrible. The man didn't now what hit him. I know that the man who delivered this package was not one of our usual supplier agents. I can't believe this, Mr. Watkins. I'm sorry to tell you this. I might have said too much."

"No, this is a secure line. Well, that is unfortunate. I'd be interested to know what sort of vehicle and toxin and whatnot got into him. Frankly, I'm not too excited by the news."

"Oh?"

"The man's been hateful to too many people and you ought to just ship him back to Washington."

The man rang off and Watkins took his time getting back to his office, knowing that Peter was there for a similar reason.

Peter sat at the edge of Watkin's desk, leafing through a document that Watkins had put aside.

Watkins marched up to Reed and grabbed it out of his hand. "If you don't mind," he said with a snap in his voice.

"I'm sorry. Force of habit."

"You have been given a discharge. Why are you here still?"

"I can't tear myself away, Watkins. I'm dying to find out what's new."

"No, nothing to talk about. I'm not interested in the gossip factory here in these parts."

Peter stood up and shrugged. "Ok, fine. I want to

tell you that I've sent a text to Elena Ramos."

"Who?" Watkins looked at him with a testy look on his face. Then his face cleared. "Oh, that girl. She's the one who we think is Revenor's mistress."

"Yes."

"And you texted her?"

"Yes. I told her the engagement was off."

"What did you do that for?"

"Because I'm out of the MI5 and now I'm releasing all the people I've had to hang out with. Stands to reason, doesn't it?"

"Oh, hell. Well, if you needed to that is fine. We will have to find a way to Revenor without your help."

"Good."

"I've had a visit from Moorhead, by the way," Watkins said, unwilling to let Peter go so soon.

"Oh, him."

"He said that Perkins was a bad egg."

"I could have told you that and I recall that I mentioned he was not trustworthy when we saw him sometime ago."

"I was not about to agree then but now I'm seeing this is true. I think that the Americans have got a few bad eggs in their basket and we need to stay clear of them."

"I don't much care, Watkins. I'm off now."

"No, it isn't as easy as that, really. I think since you have got a lot of work done with this Revenor case, you need to stay in as our consultant."

"Consultant?" Peter's eyes widened.

"Yes."

Peter said nothing.

"Moorhead has only been with us for a few years. He won't be as good yet. I suggest you and he get together - or, well through whatever channels you two have had to talk. I'm fearing that Moorhead will be the one they'll think is the engineer to Perkins' demise."

'Oh so the man finally croaked."

"He got poisoned today."

Peter again said nothing.

"Will you stay on for a consultancy post? I won't make you go in and do any operative missions. You need to be on call for whatever reason."

"Sorry, Watkins. I need to be out of your hair. I've got more unhappy news to tell YOU."

"Oh God. What more?"

"My prospective father-in-law has been murdered. Stabbed. In the hotel where he and his wife are staying."

"Damn."

"Yes, damn."

"Whatever for?"

"I'm afraid he worked for Perkins and he might have let something on and Perkins and he got the bad end of things."

Watkins stared at Peter. "I've not heard this about the man - what's his name?"

"Bartholomew. Leo Bartholomew."

"Oh." Watkins sat down finally and put a hand over his brow. "This is your or was your prospective father-in-law? Not Elena's father, though?"

"No. My - er - future bride is his - Leo's - daughter. She's the one I mentioned to you about. The parents were in town for his presentation at the Royal College of Surgeons. He gave his paper, then he went off and met a man and passed a document. One of my men spied them talking and then got a picture of them both. Bartholomew isn't anyone I've heard was in the

CIA. I can't imagine why he got himself in this situation."

"He's not in the CIA?"

"I don't know for a fact that he is. Nor do we know if he's in with the Soviets. I am not sure why he, a noted surgeon, would even want to get involved with this sort of thing. His wife is in hysterics and hurling expletives at everyone, if she's not taking any Xanax. His daughter is in shock and she could possibly be a target as well."

"Target? Why?"

"Because she's my girl." Peter's words came out evenly, as though he were explaining it to a five year old boy.

"Well, this is something I've not expected. If Perkins were someone who Bartholomew knew and worked in the CIA together, what sort of operation would they be doing?"

"I don't now yet. I suppose the Revenor case is a good reason. Everyone wants to meet Max Revenor. Except me, now. But I'm told Revenor has his talons everywhere. You tell me, Watkins."

"All I can say is that Revenor is being supported by a short list of organizations to make sure that London gets into the brink and we are now getting an American surgeon in the news which will definitely hamper any work we have been doing, am I right?"

"Yes."

"Well we have somehow got Perkins out and he won't be a bother to us."

"You think that is all we need, his deletion?"

"I think that is a good start. Let me be clear, Peter, we don't want those bad eggs in the CIA getting in the middle of our own stuff. London will never get into this sort of horrid scene where all hell breaks loose in it. It won't be pretty and we will be the laughingstock of all the world."

"I understand. But we - well," Peter scratched his head. "I'll have to - we - will have to think about this."

""I'll say one thing. We need to lay low for now. I don't give a shit if there's a stupid house party somewhere in Maidenhead - Revenor is now the real target and if anyone of these assholes who want to get him to do Hell in London we can and will find them."

Peter's eyes narrowed. "I see. Let the man and the CIA figure this whole problem out?"

"I think we need to stay out of sight for now. I'll make sure Moorhead and his girl go dark for a while."

"Fine."

"In the meantime, you be the solicitous boyfriend

of the family and see how you can handle getting the man's body out of this country, hopefully along with his daughter and wife."

"Hm."

"I insist on it, Peter. I don't want to have any more tourists and their kin getting in the crossfire."

"I''m going to do that. You won't hear from me unless you call the number we agreed upon."

"Good. Be scarce now."

Chapter Thirty-Three

Moorhead came to Peter's Notting Hill flat to deliver another box of Scotch after being summoned by Peter himself. They met at the back door with Moorhead bearing a box of the Scotch.

"How are things?" Peter asked.

"Margo and I are having a good weekend this weekend. Lots of plans for hiking and fishing and all that."

"Well, that's good."

"I'm a bit at a crossroads, old chap."

"With what?"

"I'm thinking that the people who work with Perkins got to Bartholomew for something and it isn't quite that obvious to me why he had to kill Bartholomew."

"It could be that Bartholomew said or did something that Perkins didn't like. We know that Perkins killed Bartholomew no problem there, don't you agree?"

"Yes." Moorhead lifted the lid to the box of Scotch. "Here's to a lot of good evenings with the liquid in your glass."

"Thanks, I'm looking forward to it."

"When are you all departing for the States?"

"I'm not sure yet. Mrs B isn't getting too much

cooperation with the authorities to release her husband's body. I'm sure it will happen."

"I am sure it will. You won't be seeing me again, I don't think."

"I don't know."

"You need to get out and forget about this whole thing."

"I'm a bit apprehensive about going to the USA actually."

"Oh all those CIA chaps."

"Yes."

"Then take the family and hang out in Ibiza or whatever place might be great. I wouldn't wish to live out my retirement in the USA. Lots of problems there and the CIA is filled with snakes."

Peter sighed and looked at him. "I'm not sure there are any places to live that will be good enough for me and my girl and my kid."

"I'm sad - I have my own dreams, Peter old son. I'm afraid I'll become a gnarled old thing in this MI5 place."

"I'd suggest you have a flaring love affair with Margo and get the hell out when you can." Peter spoke with a slight smile.

Moorhead lifted his head. "You think that will make a difference? The place has everyone having flings everywhere."

"Yes, I am sad to agree with that."

"Look, I'll try to do what I can to help you but I would merely go dark somewhere and well…" Moorhead's voice trailed off. After a pause, he said firmly, "What if we did this? Let's say you and your girl and your kid flew out of someplace and then the plane went down in the Bermuda Triangle and you never were found. How does that sound?"

Peter looked amazedly at him. "I don't know why I didn't think that."

"Ha, that is quite interesting - it just popped into my head."

"Good idea."

"Now who's going to get that word out that you've gone off and died out of the world?"

"You." Peter smiled at him with almost a boyish air.

"Oh." Moorhead said falling short.

"Oh, Moorhead, if you ran the world it would be so much more beautiful."

They both laughed.

Chapter Thirty-Four

The red eye to New York was not quite full. In fact, the passenger list was not long and check in was a breeze for once. The pilot and his crew huddled in the back of the plane where the coffee was served. No one spoke. No one said anything about the people that sat in their seats in the front of the cabin.

One of the passengers stood to put something in the overhead compartment. That man was with a woman who looked plain in her dark hair and spectacles. The stewardess remembered their names - Mr. and Mrs. Peter Reed. They had carry-on baggage and they also had passports that showed they were from the USA and the UK.

She observed the two talking but noticed they had not been that eager to talk much. The woman and her husband put on their seatbelt and then settled back to read. He was reading a book that the stewardess recognized as written by Ernest Hemingway. The wife was reading a Vogue magazine which she might have bought from the shop in the airport.

The other passengers included a solitary man in a Burberry cap, and wore a Mackintosh. He was about to light a cigar but the stewardess shushed him. He begged pardon and kept his cigar in his inside pocket. Then there was a woman who looked as though she was a student, her carry-on bag was a back pack and she held an iPod in her hand and earbuds were in her ears. She ignored the stewardess' preflight instructions and kept looking down at her book about Stephen Jobs. The last person on the flight was a tall and muscular man who carried a briefcase - a cloth one - that he kept under the seat. He seemed to be affable and asked her whether he could get a small glass of scotch. She gave him a smile and told him to wait.

After the instructions were read, the stewardess sat down in her own seat close to the pilot's cabin.

The pilot and co-pilot gave each other the thumbs up inside the captain's cabin. The stewardess smiled as she passed the passengers, noting where everyone was seated.

The flight took off without much fanfare, and finally the fasten seatbelt sign went off.

The night sky was clear to the pilot. It seemed quite like any flight. The airplane was well fueled. No other issues were seen by the air traffic control personnel. The tall man got up to find the water closet and shut the door. The others had settled down for the flight to New York City.

"I'm putting this on auto." The Captain spoke. "I need to go to the john. Be back in a while."

"Ok." His copilot said.

The stewardess went to get her cart which would distribute drinks and snacks. Her job was going to be easy, she thought. When she looked over the passengers, she noted that the tall man had not yet returned to his seat. She decided to make his scotch last in her list of drinks to serve.

She went down towards the front and then saw that the Reeds were gone. She decided that they both were in the water closet so she didn't think much about it.

The pilot never came back. The copilot looked worried but didn't say anything. After a few minutes, the door opened behind him. "Time you got back." said the copilot.

No answer. The copilot made a move to turn around and a hand went over his head, then he felt something come over his neck. He looked around only to catch the figure of the tall man who had requested a glass of scotch stand behind him. In one swift motion he garroted the pilot. The copilot fell out of his chair, dead.

The plane listed in and out of control. Inside the

cabin, the glasses tumbled over and the passengers started to call out in fright. "Please keep your seatbelt fastened." Said the stewardess to them. She frantically turned around to go into the pilot's cabin. She found the copilot lifeless on the floor, blood pulsing out into a hazy pool on the carpet.

Down in the cargo hold, Peter and Rebecca stood putting on their parachute gear. He looked at her questioningly. "You ok?"

"Yes. I am scared but I will be fine."

"That man should be right behind us."

"Peter, this is too - "

"I know but I explained everything to you. It's our only way out."

Rebecca nodded. He took her close and kissed her. "If I could do it any other way, my love, I would. The agency knows and they agree."

They both stepped forward to the latched door and Peter opened it easily. The plane listed slowly and Peter held on to the door with one hand and to Rebecca with the other. A noise sounded behind them. It was the tall man.

"Hey. I've made everything happen. You both need to get out now."

"Good. We'll never see you again."

"Fine. Go, go."

Rebecca and Peter clasped hands and they both jumped into the darkness below. Outside the plane two figures jumped off the cargo hold. Both held on to each other. They fell for a few hundred yards and then a parachute came out to steady them both. They fell in a soft breeze and disappeared into the dark waters below.

Back inside the captain's cabin of the airplane, the

stewardess let out a scream. The pilot came in and saw

the dead body. "What happened?"

.

Chapter Thirty-Five

In Connecticut, Sophia Bartholomew's telephone kept ringing. She ignored it and tried to concentrate on her newspaper. Finally, her brother's voice came to her ears. "What the hell are you doing, girl?"

"What do you mean?" She asked.

"It's this news. Rebecca and her boyfriend. They crashed over th the Atlantic."

The telephone rang. "Answer it, Sophia."

She rose to answer it. "Hello." Her voice sounded hollow.

"Mrs. Bartholomew, it's the British embassy in Washington, D.C."

"Yes?"

"We have some bad news. Your daughter and her boyfriend Peter Reed crashed over the Atlantic."

"Yes, I heard."

"We are now in the process of recovery. We will let you know when we find their remains."

"Thank you."

Dick, her brother, saw her drop the phone and go back to her seat. "You need to take something for this, Sophia."

"I'm not sure I care, Dick."

"No, I know you're hurting. But you need to take some meds or eat."

"I'll be fine."

Chapter Thirty-Six

The wet streets of Hamburg were empty that early

morning as a small white Fiat emerged from under the

bridge. The driver was clad in a dark green parka and

wore a tweed cap. He looked as though he had not

shaved for days. Beside him was a woman who had dark

hair and wore a similar parka. She was wearing a brown

woolen scarf that shielded the lower part of her face.

"Only a few more miles," murmured the man to her.

"I'm not worried."

"I am glad. You don't regret this at all." The statement was really a question.

"No." Came the answer.

He glanced at her face and she was staring ahead, her eyes unseeing. A feeling of guilt passed through him. "I am so very sorry. You and I, we –"

"No, it's fine. I don't know why we can't start this new thing."

"I've got to keep us dark for a while. Maybe forever."

"No, it's fine." She repeated.

"I think you and I need to discuss this."

"I think it might be dangerous."

"We are newlyweds, and I am your husband Michael Brun and you are Maren Brun, my wife. We will be living here for the foreseeable future. Our house is

somewhere nearby. We will be like any newlywed but
we won't act like it. You will be pregnant as you really
are and when you are about seven months along we will
leave to go on a pregnancy honeymoon. It's all the rage,
I hear." Michael, who was Peter, smiled ironically.
Elise smiled as well, then she tried to breathe because
she had stopped breathing for the reason that she was
terrified. "Sounds good."
Michael said nothing but concentrated on the road.
"I guess I won't be able to - "
"No," he read her mind. She was referring to her
mother who did not know she was still alive.

The plane crash was over the waters of the North Sea.
Rebecca and Peter jumped off the plane as it started to
veer out of control, and clung to each other until their

parachutes deployed. Rebecca, never having done this before, was stalwart in keeping her eyes focused on Peter who kept her steady. He got to the water first and quickly held up his arms to catch Rebecca as she fell into his arms. Both had to struggle getting out of their parachutes which was no mean feat. The quick release of the straps that went round their bodies helped and both were met by a lone fishing boat that Moorhead ordered just for their escape.

The fisherman had a German accent and spoke sharply, "You are a few minutes late, Herr Brun."

"My apologies." Peter smiled as he helped Rebecca climb on to the boat. "Meet my wife, Maren. This is - ?"

"Call me Frigo," came the gruff reply.

"Hello," she said, trying to catch her breath.

"Hallo,"

"We need to collect the parachutes and dispose of them." Peter said.

"No need to worry," spoke the fisherman. "My assistant Gossberg will attend to disposing of it. Moorhead had everything planned."

"I'll have to send the man a present for his birthday," Peter said with a half-smile directed at Rebecca.

"That would be good."

The boat was a large enough size that the couple could go down below deck to get their wet clothes off and change into new ones that Moorhead also had ready for them.

"Let's get this show on the road," spoke Peter.

"Ok." Rebecca replied, her voice still shaking.

He looked at her with concern. "You aren't feeling too bad, are you?"

"No, not really."

"It was the only way, Rebecca."

She took in a deep breath and smiled bravely at him. "I am fine, I really am." But inside she felt as though she was still flying over an abyss that threatened her existence. All her past was over and this new life she was leading with Peter was going to be almost as though she and he were writing another story for themselves.

He decided not to press her too much. He wanted her and knew that it was not going to be easy if he remained a man with a covert occupation. They got their wet clothes put away and heard the motor start and then felt the boat move slowly over the dark ocean.

Chapter Thirty-Seven

CHAPTER THIRTY-SEVEN

In London, the offices of Watkins *et al.* were buzzing

about the death of Peter Reed.   Watkins demanded

Moorhead to show up at his office immediately. The

man came in looking as though he was awakened from a

fitful sleep, and had not shaven his face at all for a few

days. This enraged Watkins even more.

"What sort of appearance is this, Moorhead? I have never seen you look this shabby." Watkins eyes flickered over the taller man's visage.

Moorhead stood on one foot and smiled sleepily. "I was on night duty, sir. I am sorry I don't look well. Is there something you wanted me to discuss with you?"

"This," he threw the newspaper at him.

Moorhead caught it and spread it out for him to read. The words on the headline read "BREXIT IS NOT NO DEAL."

Moorhead read it aloud. Watkins roared, "No, man, the

stuff on the bottom corner, about the disappearance of a
British Airways jet over the North Sea!"

Moorhead scanned the newspaper and then he said,
"Oh!" He kept on reading it. "It says that this jet plane
went dark around twelve midnight and the air traffic
controllers lost any communication a few minutes before
that happened. So, what gives?" His eyes were innocent
and yet concerned.

"That had a flight manifest and one of the passengers
was Peter Reed," spat out Watkins.

"Peter Reed?" Moorhead asked incredulously. "Our
Peter Reed?"

"And that's not all, Rebecca Bartholomew was in this

flight as well!" Watkins turned around and paced the floor in front of Moorhead. "What tomfoolery is that Reed doing? I knew he wanted to leave MI5. But this," he turned again to face Moorhead. "I can't in full conscience think that this was something he hatched up to get himself out of the service. This is treason I think!"

Moorhead looked nervous. "Treason? No, I don't want to think!"

"Oh you don't want to think, eh?" Watkins was fairly dancing with anger. "I have to - what do I do, tell me, I can't tell the people upstairs this was something I had discussed with Reed. He said he wanted to quit. And now he's apparently disappeared into the crash of a British Airways jet! It won't do, Moorhead. They'll be scouring the North Sea for this plane, and they'll find his body and that of hers, I suppose."

"It will happen, Mr. Watkins. They've tried to elope. They had to. It was something couples in love do all the time."

"I don't believe he was ever in love with her."

"I think you're wrong. Yes, I do."

"Well, I don't know – those waters are dangerous. I can't think anymore what to say to them."

"I won't tell them any more than you know, Mr. Watkins."

"Yes, well, I can't really speculate. That's not

something I can do."

"True. True." Moorhead felt the beard on his jaw and thought that it was time to get out of this situation. "I'm – ah – needing to get back to – ah – "

Watkins looked at him and his face cleared somewhat. "Ok, well, you had better be close by if these bastards upstairs start asking questions."

"Yes, sir!" Moorhead beat a hasty retreat and disappeared out of the office.

#

Outside, Moorhead shook his head as though he was shaking off a bad dream. He looked around and saw that the traffic had become thick and he was grateful enough. He decided to take a bus down to Baker Street whereupon he alighted and got into the Pub.

"Hey Moorhead, what are you up to today?" Greeted the barkeep as he saw Moorhead enter.

"Oh, nothing much. How are you, Grady?"

"It's an early morning. The breakfast crowd is coming round. They'll be needing you to do some more liquor accounts. We're low on scotch and some of the beer we're pouring." Grady said, wiping the bar with a white towel.

"Will do. Is – ah – Margot around?"

"She's in the back."

"Oh, fine." Moorhead decided not to visit the back but instead went upstairs to the second floor where he had an office that was completely in disarray due to a lack of anyone who cared to look after his job. He closed the door and took a seat and then felt totally sick.

Margot entered his office and found Moorhead doubled over in his chair. "What is happening!" She exclaimed and went over and bent over his figure.

"Oh, it's you." Moorhead finally said. His face looked blank. "I'm fine."

"No you're not." She said firmly.

"I am fine. Now what do you want?"

She went over and closed the door and then fairly tiptoed to his side. "You found out didn't you?"

"What?"

"That thing,"

"What thing?"

"Oh, tosh, you know what I mean!"

He looked at her meaningfully and held a hand over his right ear and cupped it. Margot looked as though she was caught unawares. "Oh." She went looking for a chair to sit in. "My dear Moorhead, I needed to ask you what we need to do about the water bill this month. It's really got us worried."

"Why? It's been paid."

"No, not according to the water people. It's seemingly overdue, according to the new bill we got yesterday."

Moorhead shook his head and then rose, taking her arm and then fairly shoving her out the door. "Why don't we go for a walk, shall we?"

"Wait, I need my coat."

"It's not cold outside." He said and shuffled her off to the back stairs.

They went for the Green and walked fast. This was the only way that they could talk freely.

Margot tried to keep up with his long stride. "Look, what is happening. I saw the newspaper."

"They've been – the plane crashed and both are presumed missing or dead. That's all."

"I see. But what about – it's too – "

"What is too what?"

"I can't but help thinking these upstairs people will be taking this as another exit strategy that many other old spies do to get away from the Company you see."

"Well, so what."

"You mean it's alright to do it?"

"I think they know it is and they won't be asking any more questions."

"Damn, what if I did that?"

He stopped and held her by the arms. "No, I won't allow it."

"Oh I was just jesting."

"Not even in jest. Look you will be in this thing for a while and then you'll plead something or other, whatever it might be but you aren't jumping off a plane." He looked quite frightening as he spoke. She looked nervously at him.

"I guess – well ok, fine. No planes for me."

"I'm feeling a bit poorly though, Margot. I feel quite sick, actually. I'm worried sick over that man. He's been like a big brother to me. Now I won't ever see him again."

She looked sad and felt a pang of pity for Moorhead. "Look, I'm sure it will be alright. He's a grown man. And he'll take care of himself. It will be fine really it will."

Moorhead strode along again and she walked again trying to match step for step. He sighed again and felt a drop of rain on his face. "It's starting to rain. Should we go back?" She asked.

"No, I'm in no mood to go back. It's all a bit stupid now. I don't know why I'm even in this job. I think I got myself into a pickle, Margot. I surely am in a pickle."

"No I can't believe you are saying that."

"I'm thinking there's nobody better than Reed. Now he's gone. All because of a girl named Rebecca."

"Well, she was a stunner, wasn't she?"

"I suppose."

"I think that somehow someone in the Company needs to think about how people have to say Goodbye in a less exciting way."

"I don't know. They're all stuck in the old days – there's hardly anyone there who'll do something to get people off without getting them in trouble for leaving."

Margot sighed. She started to feel more raindrops on her bare arms. "Look, we had better get back. I'm getting drenched – "

"Oh ok." They stopped and then took another route to get back to the Pub.

The next day sometime after the lunch crowd had faded away, a lone tall man in a rumpled raincoat came in and amble over to the far length of the bar. The barkeep glanced up. "Be with y' in a sec," he called out.

"Fine. I'll have a long necked Ampersand and keep it coming," said the stranger.

The barkeep looked at him and then went back to fetch the beer. There was something in the man's manner that reminded him of someone. Then it struck him. It was him. The man who had gone off into hiding. They never heard of him again.

"Here you are," the barkeep said with a light voice. "Any nuts or pretzels for the taking?"

"Nah. I'm fine." The man was in a good mood save for his being in a dreadfully fitting raincoat. The barkeep wondered if he merely got this out of the poor shop or stole it off a bum.

"Fine. Just tell me when you need something else."

At the same moment, Margot entered and with a rush said, "Hell with that cab, it nearly ruined my pants. Stupid idiot." She got to the bar and saw the stranger. A small quiver got her in the solar plexus. She was elated to see him. But he gave no real sign that he knew her. She threw a look at the barkeep. "Hey, I'll be in the back as usual, ok?"

"Sure."

Margot took off like a shot and took the stairs in two and finally got to the landing right where Moorhead had his door open. She did not knock but opened it and walked in. She was about to say something but she did not see him at his usual station. Instead, she saw that his

computer was on and she walked over. It was open but

the screen had dimmed. She resisted the urge to click it

open. Just then as she straightened herself, there was a

patter of footsteps up the stairs. "Hey ho," said

Moorhead, his face shaven and his eyes bright with

merriment.

"Did you see that guy downstairs, Moorhead?" Margot

asked breathlessly.

"Yes, I did."

"Was it Hemsford?"

"The same." He came to her and gave her a chuff on the

shoulder. They'd not had any real physical signs of

affection for each other but he was in fine fettle. "The man heard and he came bearing a gift."

"Gift?" Margot's lips formed an O. "Oh pray tell what it is."

"It's this." He slipped a document out of his jacket and showed it to her.

Margot looked at the document and then reviewed it again, this time her face looked exuberant.

"That's quite a piece of good news."

"They made it."

"Hallelujah."

"Well then we're going to make that archived and throw away the key."

"We can then, surely?" Her eyes were doubtful.

"No, we can. I'll be happy enough to bless them and hope one day we'll be back in some way as acquaintances."

The door creaked and in came the barkeep. "Hey what do you know?" Moorhead asked.

"A package came for you. It's from Whitehall." He handed it to Moorhead.

"Good, thank you." Moorhead recognized the writing

and put it aside. "I'll be here for a while but Margot and I will be taking off at about 4 o'clock. Need to find a good outfit for her for the reception for the Queen's 97th birthday, if you can imagine that."

The barkeep raised his eyebrows. "Is that so? Why are YOU invited?"

"We're there to keep an eye on things, that's all."

"Oh," the man smirked. "That's all. Well that's all she can command. She's old as a nut. Why does that woman still live I ask you. It's too boring. All this kerfuffle about this and that."

"Careful, Sonny," smiled Moorhead. He winked at Margot. "I'll be putting on my rented tux and squiring

Miss Margot Huxley around. I say, Margot, is that last name of yours real or what?"

She giggled. "It's not real. But I was an actress first before I came to join up. The last name turns enough heads and I get a date once in a while."

They all chuckled and gave each other a pat on the back. Margot took a glance at the document and then something in her stomach turned. "Moorhead."

"I know. Let's scram." He took off with her in tow.

Chapter Thirty-Eight

The funeral home was filled to capacity with a long line
that snaked outside the building. Mourners from all
around the area where Leo Bartholomew practiced his
surgery came to pay their respects. Inside, there were
several halls, and one of them was the chapel where his
remains lay in a silver casket. The casket was closed,
which relieved the mourners and was a comfort to
Sophia who felt still as though the world had turned

around on her and left her feeling rootless.

She stayed in another hall where there were rows of well-upholstered chairs and a video of Leo in his still pictures going round and round for those who wanted to view them. Sophia was dressed in a black suit that had a white rose on the lapel. Her face was white as a sheet and the only color she wore was her red lipstick that made her look almost unreal. Her brother Dick Smith and his wife, Mary, stayed close by and watched as Sophia stood to receive the mourners. "So good to see you, how are you?" She said in her subdued voice.

Mary turned to her husband. "I'm going to see if the girls have put all the food out for the people who wish to stay and chat."

"Good idea." Dick said without any real expression in his face. He was not sure that Sophia was needing to take another one of the pills her doctor had prescribed for her.

"Ok, you and Sophia will be ok while I'm with the other girls?"

"We'll be ok."

"Ok." She left them and let out a breath of relief.

There was a momentary lull when the line of mourners stopped as one of Leo's former patients knelt by his casket and became emotional. Dick looked at Sophia. "You ok, Sis?"

"No, not at all. I want to get out of this place." She said under her breath. "I can't believe the people who came. I think it will be hours before everyone leaves."

"It looks like that, yes."

"Well, it isn't great. I know Leo was a good surgeon but man, it is making me wish I had taken another dose. . ."

"I can stand here for you. Why don't you go and ask Mary if she needs your help."

"No, I don't want to talk to anyone. I miss my Rebecca," she started to sob.

Dick looked up imploringly at the ceiling. It was unfair. Her husband and her daughter getting killed within

weeks of each other. It wasn't fair, Lord, it wasn't fair.
Dick put an arm around Sophia and then shepherded her
out of the hall. The mourners did not take it badly, they
thought this was all a normal thing – they had not heard
about Rebecca dying in a plane crash yet. So those who
came to see Sophia and saw her leave with her brother
shrugged and looked elsewhere to find food if there was
any left to eat.

Chapter Thirty-Nine

The following week after the funeral of Leo

Bartholomew, Mr. Watkins received a visitor. The

visitor was Sir Andrew Cloche from Whitehall. This

was an unexpected visit and Mr. Watkins wished he had

chosen the grey flannel suit instead of the glen plaid one

because the latter was too modern for his taste. But, he

sighed that it was too late and Andrew Cloche was

sitting across from him. He had a rather relaxed attitude

and made no real attempt to start anything in the way of serious discussions. This alarmed Watkins all the more, for Cloche was not just your ordinary personage from Whitehall.

"I see your office had a nice spruce up, Watkins?" asked Cloche amiably.

"Yes, we had a few things we touched up." Watkins matched his tone and felt as relaxed as he could muster.

"Look, I'm a bit concerned about this matter of Peter Reed going down into the North Sea. His body has not been recovered as far as I know." The steely grey eyes of Cloche became more intense even though he was sitting as if nothing made a muscle in his body tense up.

"I am too."

"Did he have an assignation? Was he ever thinking of going over to Europe – say – for some assignment?"

"No, he doesn't tell me much. He's his own man and we let him go and do what he needs to do. He's quite good and gets results."

"Well I need to find out if he's alive or not. Will you be able to get that information to me or my man Stevens?"

"I'll see what I can do, Sir Andrew." Watkins replied. He was able to meet the steely gaze and not suffer any obvious reaction. Watkins was used to this sort of treatment. These boys from Whitehall with their Turnbull & Asser turnouts didn't make any impression on him.

"Good. And – ah – it also seems that he went with a woman. Rebecca was her name. She was there using his name. Married, it seemed. Was he marrying her? I have not heard he was attached."

"I think he was telling me he was seeing someone."

"And this woman happened to be on the plane with him."

"I am told she was there."

"And she – they were a couple. Heading out with wedding fluffery I'm thinking."

"No I do not know that. I know that he had a few other women he was interested in. I figured he was using them for cover."

Andrew Cloche sighed. "Ah, I see. He's one of those. That included that Spanish girl – Elena Something."

"Yes that was one of his covers."

"I want to see all of his reports, Watkins. Now." The voice became sharp. And Cloche got up and leaned over him, his face red with menace. "I'm not happy about our best agent getting out of the world and ending up in the North Sea. With a woman who is a wife of his which I do not see at all as being true. No record of him marrying this women. No idea at all what she is to him. I do not like this one iota."

Watkins leaned back, his jaw pressed down against his tie and swallowed hard. "Look, I'll give you what we have. Mr. Reed never said a lot. He wasn't the type to hand in a report."

"What? Is this true? How the devil did you figure anything he did and if it was ever concluded?" Andrew Cloche swung around and paced the floor. "Damn, if he's defected I'll be – " He swung around again. "I'm not happy Watkins. You have to find out what this Peter Reed did and if he is still in the bottom of the North Sea. Then I want his carcase taken out and put on a slab and identified. Is that understood?"

At that moment, Moorhead rushed in and then gasped at the scene, whereupon he stood straight as a ramrod and nodded. "Hello, Sir Andrew."

"Who are you?"

"Moorhead. Alex Moorhead." He proffered a hand but Cloche did not take it. "I'm here to – ah - I can come back."

Cloche left but not before he gave Watkins a look.

Watkins fairly sank in his chair and took out a handkerchief. He wiped his sweating brow. "Glad you came Moorhead."

"I'm glad the guy doesn't remember me." Moorhead said cheerfully.

"I don't want to know. Look what did you want?"

"I've got news."

"Good, I hope."

"Well, I think it's good."

"Let's hear it."

Moorhead went to the man's desk and sat in the chair that was occupied by Cloche. "There's some rumour in the CIA that they wanted Reed to get hit."

Watkins looked at him and blinked. "Oh?"

"Don't know if it's true. That CIA man – whoever he

was – Perkins – yes – well – he wanted someone to take Reed out. They were to have done it the night that he and – that he left on that flight."

"Good show." Watkins laughed. "I'm happy now."

"That makes you happy?"

"Yes. I can – well you have this somewhere in black and white, correct?"

"Yes. I have it. But it's now in your safe. I gave it to your girl."

"Good. I'll be glad to tell Cloche this. He was fit to be tied."

"Good," echoed Moorhead. "I'll say this – this was not unexpected. Perkins hated Reed. And Reed was aware of it. I am also told that the CIA is muddy as hell these days. Too many people handling things and nobody managing it the right way. The usual back and forth."

"That is why they're all going to blazes, soon, I guess."

Watkins got up and blew his nose into his handkerchief. "Well, that's fine. I won't ask you what transpired on that flight. I'll give Reed the freedom to go and find his own way out of the Company. I'll say this though, if he ever got tired of that woman he wants it will be dashed hard for him to figure out where to get back here."

"No, I think he's known this was the end of the line and he'll be a yokel someday pumping gas for some

Portuguese filling station." Moorhead laughed softly.

"It's a sad life."

"Why do it then, Mr. Watkins?" Moorhead asked, his eyes thoughtful on his superior.

"It's for Her Majesty's Secret Service."

"Oh that old thing."

"Yes. She has to be obeyed."

"Well. . ."

"Now, let's talk about Revenor. I am hoping to find out that you've got him squarely in your sights."

Watkins sat down again and looked tiredly at Moorhead who gave him a low key update.

Chapter Forty

The roar of the surf awakened Maren, as she slept in the
arms of Michael. They were in a large king sized bed, in
a well-appointed bedroom. There was a small fire in the
fireplace that Michael started the night before and they
made love in the firelight. They were exhausted and fell
asleep with their hearts still beating fast at the passion
that passed between them. Elise's eyes flickered open

and she did not immediately recognize their surroundings. Michael, his eyes still closed, sensed her body clench and he murmured, "No worrying, my love. Everything is good now."

"Yes, I think it's good." But there was a hint of doubt in her voice, still and small as it was. It was as though she didn't wish to break the spell of their quiet togetherness.

"No it IS good." He pulled her closer. "We have the house – I paid for it many years ago when I planned to leave the service in the later years of my career there. Everyone knows me as Michael and they will be happy to meet you finally."

Maren turned her glowing face to his. "Really? You already had this planned?"

He tapped the tip of her nose with a chuckle. "I was very much prepared to leave that place. It sucks you dry, this work of mine – or what it was a work of mine. I wanted to find a place where I could relax, be me, be totally out of that culture. I don't think anyone here knows that I had another job or that I was anything but me, a German citizen who liked to travel for business. Nothing out of the ordinary."

"I don't know what you did – all I know is that I fell for you hard and you said you would take care of everything, of me – and everything."

"I did and I will."

"Will we stay here forever?"

"It depends." Michael said with a serious face. "I am already thinking that some asshole in the north American continent is trying to find out about me and how I got killed in an airplane crash."

A shadow of fear crossed Elise's face. "We aren't totally free, then."

"I think we will be what my father used to call wanderers. I don't expect - " He clapped his hand over his forehead. "Damn, I had forgotten about the baby.'

"Yes, you did." Elise laughed softly. "Well, you and I are going to be a happy family of three."

"Don't have to worry for a while though. We have

enough people here who used to be in the service and want to keep this place out of the radar of these bastards who want to keep making war and spreading lies everywhere just to make their world go round and round."

Elise drew the covers over her naked shoulders and snuggled next to him. His body was warm against hers and they embraced once again. They shared a kiss that went on forever. Then in the early light of day they made love with a fierceness that made them shudder with ecstasy.

Chapter Forty-One

THE PENTAGON, UNITED STATES

The last person to enter the conference room was a man who carried a thin aluminum briefcase. Everyone looked at him with consternation on their faces. He looked undisturbed. He was the one they all wanted to listen to. He needed to tell them what happened. And he looked as though he had answers.

The meeting started. Outside, the snow was driving. The cherry blossoms trees that adorned the city were all covered with thick snow globules and the traffic was snarled. A few snow plows were out. There were many who decided to take the public transportation. The man who came in to the meeting did not have any outer indications that he had been disturbed by the snowstorm.

"Now that General Patrick is here," intoned the man at the head of the table. "we can all start. I appreciate everyone showing up despite the blizzard-like conditions."

"Thanks, General Hennesy." General Patrick said, his pinched face cracking a brief smile.

"We want to have the information and get this over with." Said another person, his thick person was clothed in a uniform that could not entirely keep all of his bulk comfortable.

"So," General Patrick said in preamble. "This is what we know. General Jack Perkins was found dead in an apparent murder by anthrax poisoning. His office in London was screened. The man who delivered the envelope was not identified too well and he left without being noticed."

"What? That is unimaginable." Spoke another.

""That is unfortunate," spoke Patrick. "we know that the man worked for a printer. We know that Perkins was someone who ordered this item that the printer said he did. At least, there was a paper trail and Perkins signed off on it."

A general dissatisfied murmur went round the room.

"Cut to the chase, man." Ordered Hennesy.

"Fine. Let me say that Perkins was a bastard and he worked for the Soviets. His murder was not something we predicted but someone was on top of this and to this man we owe a great deal of thanks."

"Oh, my God." Hennesy said. His eyes were almost dark with indescribable disappointment.

"No one knew he was working for the Soviets?" Asked

a man who was at the other end of the table. His face was nondescript.

"I think someone knew."

"So what else do we know?"

"I found out that Perkins ordered a hit on one Peter Reed, an MI5 agents."

"This Peter Reed, that the man who died in the plane accident?" Asked a man who held a handkerchief to his mouth as he just sneezed.

"Yes, that's the one."

"Why the hell kill Reed for?"

"We know why.   Reed and Perkins hated each other on sight. Perkins thought Reed found something out and so he wanted Reed to die."

"So this Perkins is dead. Reed is dead. The secret of Perkins is now what, is it just something for us to try to chase after?" Hennesy demanded.

"No, - well, not exactly," said the man with the nondescript face.

"What do you mean?"

"We chase after it and then we nip it in the bud. We eliminate all of Perkin's people and that is all."

"Hell." Another man said, his face looking around, as though he couldn't believe the coldness of this statement.

"What else do we do?"

"Ok so this is all. I have no wish to say anything to MI5 do we agree?"

There was a palpable silence. Then they all went around the table and said "Agreed."

THE END

www.ingramcontent.com/pod-product-compliance
Lightning Source LLC
Chambersburg PA
CBHW020651110726
47901CB00001B/134